I0761934

# *A Family's Spirit*

# *A Family's Spirit*

Karyl Hall &
Carolyn Graham

Carmel, California

October 2018

This is a work of fiction. Names, characters, places, and incidents are the product of the authors' imagination or are used fictitiously, and any resemblance to any actual person, living or dead, events, or locales is entirely coincidental.

A Family's Spirit



Interior illustrations by Natalie Bieser
Cover Illustrations by Carolyn Graham



ISBN: 978-1-7325450-0-7

Printed in the United States

# *TABLE OF CONTENTS*

# ***Publisher's Note***

When I met with Karyl after reading *A Family's Spirit,* she was visibly surprised that I liked her book; surprised that I had even read it. She had been discouraged at the lack of attention the book received when it was first published in 2000. In fact, the lack of response had been so disappointing that my pleasure with and excitement over the book had her near to tears.

I suggested to Karyl that she reissue her book because her stories and how she told them would be meaningful to parents and children alike. For millennia, parents have recounted myths of their culture, and later read stories that would help their children grow their minds. Not just their intellect, but their character. We have to get back to that.

So parents - and grandparents and other members of the family - turn off the television, put down the cellphone, and talk to - and with - your children. Read to them. Get them interested in words and stories. You've made a good start by picking up *A Family's Spirit.*

Tony Seton
Carmel, California

*Karyl Hall & Carolyn Graham*

# AUTHOR'S NOTE

One of the saddest times of my life was when this book was completed. It meant that I had to say goodbye to all the characters I had come to love, as well as say goodbye to my co-author, who lived a distance away. Many lessons for today's world are captured between these covers.

This book has appeal for both children and adults. It is rich with sweet and touching stories, tales of the trials and triumphs of a mouse family. Mother Mouse is a widow with five children. Father Mouse has recently died, leaving the family to grapple with missing him and challenges of growing-up in his absence. They rise to the occasion, and many life lessons are learned in this truly magical year.

Karyl Hall
Carmel, California

*Karyl Hall & Carolyn Graham*

# *I - Shiver Me Timbers!*

It had been a beautiful Saturday morning following a blustery storm. A few weeks ago Roscoe had found a raft, a relic of the previous summer, washed up on the bank of the stream. Scrambling down from the bridge, he had pulled it to higher ground, tying it by an old frayed rope to the rickety pier.

What a find!

He didn't know at the time exactly what he would do with it, but there was no doubt in his mind that he would think of something one day.

And today was that day.

"Yo, ho, ho," muttered Roscoe under his breath.

He looked around with what he hoped was a casual air.

He knew Mother had started Spring cleaning, for all the

pillows and quilts and feather mattresses were outside for airing, and he could hear the faint swish of mop and broom through the open windows. Sarah already had a start on the week's baking, Roberta had been sent on an errand, and an unwilling Sam had been dragged from his room and was cleaning winter debris from the garden, placing it in the big bin for Mr. Hedgehog to haul off.

Roscoe smiled. Sam didn't look too happy.

The smile disappeared almost immediately. If he was going to avoid work, he'd better get away quickly.

"Roscoe!" came his mother's impatient call.

Roscoe's heart sank. For just a second he considered pretending that he had not heard, then sighed and turned around.

"Yes, Mother?" he said with a despondent look.

"I want you to watch Skitch, Roscoe -- he is completely underfoot," she called from an upstairs window.

Roscoe gazed at his mother, who was wearing an apron and had a large scarf tied around her head to keep the dust out of her fur. She looked slightly frazzled.

"Do I have to, Mother? I was just -"

"Roscoe," said Mother tartly, "I am cleaning, Sarah is baking, Roberta is off after early berries, and Sam is cleaning the garden." She paused. "Would you rather dig the vegetable bed?"

"No, that's okay," responded Roscoe hastily. "I'll take

Skitch -- we can go play somewhere."

"I thought so," muttered Mother Mouse, drawing her head inside.

"Oh rats!" said Roscoe.

As if he had been awaiting his cue, Baby Skitch toddled around from the back of the house and beamed up at Roscoe.

"I'll bet Roberta's up in some old tree now, eating all the berries," said Roscoe rebelliously. "And if Mother's waiting for Sam to clear the garden she can forget about planting until next year." He kicked the dirt.

Roscoe gazed at Skitch standing before him in anticipation. Baby thought maybe he'd get a ride in the wheelbarrow.

Roscoe was concentrating on how to salvage the day.

Gradually little Skitch came into focus, and Roscoe realized with rising enthusiasm that he was looking at not the despoiler of his day, but, rather -- crew!

Roscoe, spirits restored, smiled widely at Skitch.

"Come on fur ball!" he said.

Skitch was happy to see Roscoe smiling again. He was ready to go wherever his big brother wanted to take him.

Headed towards the stream, Roscoe gave occasional backward glances to make sure that Mother was not looking.

Not that he thought he was doing anything wrong, he

assured himself.

It was just that Mother was sometimes too cautious.

The raft was tethered to the old pier, just where he had left it. A bit disconcerted by the fact that it was now floating on the water rather than lying on the bank, Roscoe gazed at the swollen stream with mild anxiety.

The current seemed much quicker down close than it had appeared from a distance. He noticed small leaves and twigs eddying in whirlpools, then quickly breaking away to rush on downstream.

It'll be okay, he thought. He began making eye patches for himself and Skitch.

"Hey!"

Roscoe whirled and, to his annoyance, saw his sister Roberta running towards them.

"What are you doing here?" he demanded when she had caught up to them. "I thought you were supposed to be picking berries."

"I was. I finished and I had so many pails, Mother said I could go and play for a while. Then I saw you and Skitch and I cut across the meadow to catch up."

She saw the raft and looked at him curiously.

"What were you planning to do? Not get on that old thing, I hope!"

Roscoe had been having second thoughts, but resented

his sister's disparagement of his find.

"I had thought about it," he said.

"With Skitch?"

Roscoe became defensive. "So what? It's only a little stream. You can probably wade across it."

Still dubious, Roberta examined the paddle that Roscoe (with great foresight, he thought) had brought with them, and laughed at the eye patches he had made for Skitch and himself from leaves and reeds.

Roberta looked again at the raft and the water.

"Are you sure it's shallow enough? The water looks like it's moving kind of fast."

"Are you afraid?"

That was too much for Roberta.

"I'm coming with you," she said.

"I don't know, Roberta," Roscoe protested. "I thought it would only have to hold me and Skitch."

"Okay, so if I'm too heavy for the raft I'll just wade back to shore. Okay?"

Roscoe agreed reluctantly.

He tied the reed around Baby Skitch's head and adjusted the eye patch, then put on his own. He wished he had a peg leg, or a knife to hold between his teeth.

He'd just have to pretend.

Half carrying, half dragging Skitch, he slithered down the muddy bank.

The raft wobbled precariously until he, Skitch, and Roberta were safely on.

He looked at his crew.

"Weigh anchor!" he said.

Skitch squealed in excitement and the raft wobbled again with his enthusiastic bouncing. Roberta snorted.

"Whoa!" cried Roscoe, trying to balance himself and get Skitch settled down.

"Now, you have to sit still," he said sternly. "Do you understand? Still. You have to be still. Roberta, you're going to have to watch him."

"Well, what were you going to do if I hadn't been here?"

Roscoe ignored her, but Skitch immediately looked contrite. He knew "still." Everyone was always saying it to him.

He faced forward with a grim look on his little face, his pudgy paws on the knees of his outstretched legs.

"Okay," grunted Roscoe, working at the knot in the rope. "In a moment we'll be on the high seas!"

Finally the knot unraveled and the raft, bobbing at first against the pier, was drawn out into the wide stream.

They moved quickly but easily with the current and, despite his first misgivings, Roscoe found that he could steer pretty well with the paddle.

He relaxed.

Now and then Skitch, mesmerized by the quickly moving scenery and rushing water, glanced back at Roscoe.

Roscoe was acting very strangely indeed.

He said things like "Ahoy, matie!" and "The sailor's life for me!" and "Yo ho ho and a bottle of rum!"

Skitch knew "bottle" and looked around expectantly. Nothing was forthcoming, however, so he turned his gaze back to the water, remembering to stay still.

"Look, Skitch," said Roscoe, pointing beyond the left bank. "See the school? That's where Sam and I go every morning when you stay home with Mother."

"And over there is Mr. Possum's store," added Roberta.

"Oh, like he could care?" snickered Roscoe.

"Well, how much do you think he cares about school?" she retorted.

They passed the Beavers' house set high up on stilts, and waved to the Muskrat family who were coming from the woods with loads of firewood.

What fun! thought Skitch. First a slippery slide down the muddy hill, then bobbing around on the water, the attentions of his big brother, and now water lapping at his toes. Skitch leaned over to play in it, but remembered in time that he was to be "still" and immediately sat up again.

"Roscoe..."

"I know, I see it. I told you it would be too much with you onboard."

It seemed that the raft sat somewhat lower in the ever-widening stream now than it had at the beginning of the trip.

Am I getting close to the river? Roscoe thought with apprehension. He knew the little streams eventually fed into the big river, and they were sternly forbidden to play on the riverbank without an adult around.

And, too, he was beginning to have a little difficulty with the paddle. He looked a bit wistfully at Skitch and Roberta. It would be nice right now to have a real crew. Oh, well, at least Skitch was still.

*I told you it would be too much with you onboard.*

But Skitch was beginning to whimper. The water was cold and now he was sitting in it. Bravely he tried to refrain from wriggling, but soon his whimpering turned into little sobs, and now and then Roscoe could hear "Mama," one of the few consistently recognizable words in Skitch's limited vocabulary.

"Roberta, can't you do something?"

"I'm trying, Roscoe. It's just that the water is cold and he doesn't like it."

Just as Roscoe decided he had better head for shore, the

paddle caught on a submerged branch and was wrenched from his hand.

Recovering his balance, Roscoe gazed after it aghast.

He had almost gone with it! He was swept by an unfamiliar panic.

He quickly regained his composure, then turned to

*I told you it would be too much with you onboard.*

Roberta who was holding onto Skitch. The baby was squeaking at the top of his lungs.

"Shh! Shh!" said Roscoe, now on his knees with them and, like Roberta, one arm around Skitch and holding tight to the side of the raft.

The raft was caught in the strong current, and they were, indeed, on the river! Roscoe realized he had no control whatsoever. Suddenly the raft was captured by a small whirlpool and began spinning in smaller and smaller circles.

"Ma-ma!" squeaked Skitch.

Roberta froze.

In his panic, Roscoe remembered the leaves and twigs that swirled about and then were released to bounce about willy-nilly on the water and to rush downstream once more.

And then they were released by the whirlpool and Roscoe linked his arm with Roberta's and braced himself and Skitch for the wild ride ahead!

His heart beat so fast he felt he was choking, and he hugged Skitch tighter. With no real handholds, and nothing to grasp, the three small figures were barely able to stay aboard as the raft turned and twisted in its headlong course.

Oh, why hadn't he stayed home and helped? He thought fleetingly of Sam and Sarah. Their boring chores didn't seem so bad now. How he wished he was home peacefully digging the vegetable bed! They were at home!

Then, the raft stopped abruptly its furious rush, the back end swinging around and still bobbing. Roberta was almost flung off.

Going around a bend in the river, the raft had been

swept near enough to shore to be caught momentarily by the water rushes. But Roscoe knew that it was only a matter of seconds before they would again be swept away.

"Hold onto Skitch" he cried to Roberta.

He began paddling desperately with his paws, but could feel the current tugging at them. Just a little farther!

There!

As soon as the nearest clump of grasses was close enough, he reached out and grabbed them securely.

They were out of the current now, Roscoe saw with relief. By grabbing one clump after another, he was able to bring the raft into a harbor of sorts.

"Saved from a watery grave, me hearties," he said weakly as he surveyed the damage: their paddle was gone, he and Skitch had long ago lost their eye patches, and all of them were soaked to the skin.

Skitch had stopped crying once he realized the water was no longer rushing them along and washing over the raft, and had watched curiously as Roscoe pulled them ashore.

Maybe it would get fun again!

Roscoe's legs were rubbery as he stepped into the shallow water, holding fast to the rope that had trailed behind them. Laboriously, he pulled the raft ashore to the accompaniment of small noises of encouragement from Skitch.

Exhausted, Roscoe sat down on the grassy bank, resting a moment, then wringing out his shirt and little Skitch's as well.

The warm sun and the solid ground felt so good!

Skitch, still somewhat wet and chastened, looked up at Roscoe, who felt immediate remorse.

"Look, Skitch," he said, trying to get a smile from him, "We can tie the shirts around our heads -- there -- we'll just bring the arms around like that -- and now we're sheiks of the desert!"

Skitch peered up at him silently from the damp shirt tied around his damp head.

"All right," sighed Roscoe, removing the shirt. "We'll just wave them around until they're dry."

He sneaked a glance at Roberta, who was sitting on the grass beside them, her face tight with anger.

"So, go ahead and say it!"

"Say what?"

"Whatever you're thinking."

"I'm thinking you took us out on an old leaky raft and said the stream was shallow enough to wade in and we almost got drowned."

"What are you talking about? The raft didn't leak -- I told you it would be too much weight with you on it, too!"

"Roscoe, we weren't in the stream anymore. We were on the river."

He turned away. "Well, I didn't know we were so close to the river, or that we would go so fast," he muttered.

But Roberta was not so easily appeased.

Just then Skitch began to whimper.

"Skitch! Want to go home and get something to eat?" asked Roscoe enthusiastically, glad to change the subject.

Skitch brightened and stood up. Roscoe realized he was ravenous as well.

Must be the sea air, he thought.

The three of them set off for home, Roscoe and Roberta in stony silence. It wasn't long before Skitch sat down and, despite all of Roscoe's cajoling, refused to get up and walk. His eyelids drooped noticeably, but before he could lie down, Roscoe picked him up with a grunt and hoisted him on his shoulders.

With his brother clutching his ears, Roscoe fell into a rhythm and walked along, Skitch bouncing up and down, spirits restored.

All the familiar things of home seemed much more inviting now to Roscoe. He imagined them all seated around the dining table, with the late afternoon sun streaming through the window and the brass candlesticks on the mantel gleaming. Sam would probably be reading a book hidden in his lap, Roberta would be fidgeting and Sarah helping Mother bring in the steaming dishes from the kitchen. His mouth watered.

They jogged along.

Thinking over all that had happened from the time they slid down the muddy bank, Roscoe saw his own role as increasingly valiant and brave.

When you got right down to it, he thought, he had really saved his little brother's life.

"Just think how jealous Sam and Sarah will be when we tell them about our ride," said Roscoe.

Roberta was silent.

"And when we tell them how we were almost swept away by the river, they'll realize how brave we are."

Roberta maintained her silence.

"And just think how the kids at school -"

"Just think of what Mother will say when she hears about it!" interrupted Roberta.

At that, Roscoe was silent.

"Maybe we'd just better not say anything at all?" he suggested.

"Maybe we'd better not," Roberta agreed.

But how magnificent he had been!

He'd kept the raft afloat during the worst seas of the century!

When he lost his mast, did he give up? Never!

He had stood on the deck of his ship and braved the elements!

He had managed single-handedly to save himself, his ship and his crew!

Then the expression on Mother's face flashed once again into his mind.

Yes, it would probably be better not to mention any of this, thought Roscoe.

"Good thing Skitch can't talk," he said cheerfully.

Unaware of how the day would return to haunt him, Roscoe jogged along with Skitch, singing to himself, Roberta trudging along behind.

"Yo, ho, ho and a bottle of rum!"

# *II - THE GOLDEN RULE*

"I'm going to run away from home," announced Sarah Mouse as she and her friend Wally Mole sat in the grass at Wally's house.

Taken aback, blinking rapidly behind his large round eyeglasses, Wally just stared at her.

"It's the only thing I can think of to do," she added.

Wally still didn't know what to say. Living next door to each other, they had been best friends their entire short lives, and Wally trusted Sarah completely. If she said this was the only choice she had, then he believed it implicitly.

However, it didn't prevent him from having some misgivings.

"Are you sure, Sarah?"

"Yes, I'm sure," she answered. Actually, she hadn't been

so certain at first, but now that she had finally said it, she was.

Wally pondered the matter further.

"I don't think school will be that bad," offered Wally. "I mean, you'll be okay. I'm the one that's really dumb. Everyone else seems to know what to do. Roscoe and Homer Hedgehog and Franklin Beaver are going to go on to school in town -- Franklin wants to be an engineer -"

"I know," laughed Sarah. "He said he's tired of rowing everyone across the river, and he's going to build bridges everywhere."

Wally smiled, then continued. "And Sam -- he gets good grades all the time, and everyone loves his poems. I think he's the smartest one in the school. And you'll be fine, you're smart, too."

Wally looked glum, and Sarah sat up excitedly.

"Wally, will you come with me?"

"Wha-?"

"We can run away together, then neither of us will have to be alone. You won't have to go to school, and I won't have to leave home by myself. It's perfect, don't you see?"

"But Sarah, where will we go, and," he asked, as his stomach grumbled -- it had been a long time since lunch -- "what will we eat?"

Sarah answered him impatiently. "Oh, we can figure out where to go once we get going -- somewhere where you don't have to go to school -- and don't worry about food. I'll pack us some. You know how they carry stuff tied in a bundle on a stick? We can make those."

Wally nodded. He had only seen one in storybooks, but if Sarah said they could make them, then he was sure they could.

"I'll tell you what. You find two good sticks this afternoon and I'll do the rest. Then tomorrow morning we can leave."

"Tomorrow morning?" croaked Wally, for whom this was all still in the just-talk-about stage.

"No point in putting it off," said Sarah firmly. "It's only a week until school starts, and we want to be far away by then."

"Okay."

"Now, I'm going home, because I have stuff to plan and pack, and remember, go to bed early, because we have to be ready to leave by the time the sun comes up. I'll meet you right outside our back gate, okay?"

"Okay."

"And be quiet in the morning, because the last thing we want is for someone to hear us!"

"Okay."

Wally watched Sarah climb the low wall between their houses and run blithely inside her front door. He sat and pondered Sarah's plan until he heard his mother call him for dinner.

Wally ate slowly and methodically, trying to pack in as much as he could. He sensed that provisions might soon be in short supply. He spoke little and when, shortly afterwards, he said goodnight, his mother watched a bit anxiously as he mounted the stairs. Was he coming down with something?

Wally laid out his clothes for the next day, then climbed into bed where he tossed and turned, partly due to his confusion over his hasty decision, partly due to indigestion. Despite what he had said to Sarah, he still wasn't sure about this whole thing. Oh, he would go with her all right. Sarah held a special place in his heart, for she accepted him for who he was and had stood by him many times. He would stand by her now.

After all, what were friends for?

Sarah, meanwhile, slept soundly. After days of indecision, she had finally made up her mind as to what she was going to do, and now all troubling thoughts were gone.

The entire past week she had been marking off each day on her calendar, and now THE DAY -- the first day of school -- loomed just ahead of her. She had been in an agony of excitement and apprehension.

"What is school really like? What do you do there all day? Is it hard? What happens if you just don't feel like going? Will I like the teacher? What does she say if you make a mistake?"

Tracking down her friends, impaling them with an intense look, she had become a nuisance with all her questions.

"Oh, what are you worried about, anyway, Sarah?" Molly Beaver had asked as she tied an immense bandage around Mickey Squirrel's finger where he had cut it -- again -- whittling those little sticks of wood. "I'm going to be a doctor when I grow up, so I have to go to school to learn all about bandages and operations and -- and -- broken bones and medicine and stuff."

"I wonder what we have skin for, anyhow?" asked Mickey, gazing morosely at his finger.

"Oh," responded Molly matter-of-factly. "It's so we can't see our insides." She lowered her voice and looked at Sarah. "It's really gross in there."

"Well, I'm starting school, too, Sarah, just like you and Roberta and Molly and Megan Squirrel, and I'm not worried," said Cassie Rabbit, with a giggle. "My sisters told me all about it and I think it's going to be fun!"

Sarah had turned from them all in disgust. None of their answers satisfied her. Roscoe began teasing her by making up horror stories of what happened to students who lost their homework, couldn't learn their times tables, or forgot how to carry in addition. She listened in stony silence.

But in private, Sarah's eyes grew large and round and her lip quivered as she imagined herself in the position of one of these unfortunates.

If only Father were here, thought Sarah in misery. He could solve any problem.

But Father Mouse had died months and months ago, and Sarah felt bereft and alone.

She had turned in desperation to her twin. But Roberta -- who feared nothing and no one, who lived in the joy of the moment with her eyes perpetually crinkled in laughter -- scoffed at Sarah's fears. Roberta ran off to play and to wrest the utmost from these last days.

Now Sarah would show them all. They would be sorry when they discovered that she was gone. Maybe forever!

Sarah awoke the next day before sunrise. While the others were still sleeping, she tip-toed downstairs to the kitchen.

Her mouth watered as she fixed peanut butter and jelly sandwiches which, along with apples, and acorns for dessert, she carefully wrapped in scarves.

Then, careful to be quiet, Sarah dutifully swept the kitchen floor. This was her favorite morning chore, and the last time she would get to do it.

When she was finished and her apron hung back on its hook, she slipped out the kitchen door into the cool morning. Stars still sprinkled the sky, but it was just light enough for her to make her way down the path to the gate in the back wall. Closing it carefully and quietly behind her, she peered around.

"Wally?" she whispered.

"Here," he whispered back from the gloom.

Sarah was relieved to see that he had not forgotten the sticks, and she sat down to tie the bundles to them. Handing one to Wally and putting the other over her shoulder, she motioned to him. "Let's go."

Obediently, Wally marched down the narrow path behind her. Soon they were out in the meadow, hidden by the tall grasses.

"Did we have to leave so early?" asked Wally, still a little sleepy.

"Yes, otherwise, we couldn't have gotten away so easily. Last night Roscoe said he wanted to play Robin Hood in the woods. At least I won't have to go through that again!"

Sarah was well aware of the tendency for Roscoe's playmates to become victims in his great adventures. In fact, she remembered spending a whole afternoon tied to a willow tree because Roscoe had forgotten her there. Roscoe had apologized, but Sarah thought it was with an eye more to Mother's anger than to the ordeal he had put her through.

The sky was lightening now and as the sun rose, it became warmer and pleasant to be outside in the meadow. The dry grasses on the late August morning were still wet with dew. Birds sang in the trees, and butterflies perched on the tall wildflowers slowly opened and closed their wings, warming themselves in the early sunlight.

"Look, Wally! There's a grasshopper!"

It waved its antennae at them, then leapt away.

Wally eyed it enviously. Why couldn't he have been born a grasshopper, without a care in the world?

*Obediently, Wally marched down the narrow path behind her.*

But Sarah's thoughts were quite different. She dreamed of Roscoe and Sam and Roberta sitting around the dinner table, sadly eyeing her empty seat, and wearily toiling at all of Sarah's old chores.

How they would miss her!

Wally was sniffing the air. Something smelled good.

"I smell food," he said, adding apologetically, "I didn't have any breakfast."

"That's our lunches you smell. Well," said Sarah, looking at how high the sun had risen in the sky, "maybe we can stop and have a snack, just to keep up our strength."

Sarah pointed to an old log behind which they could sit and be hidden. Wally responded eagerly and soon had his bundle untied.

"Thith is good, Sawah" he said through a mouthful of sandwich. "I whath reawy hungwy!"

It tasted good to Sarah, too. The stick had gradually become heavier and heavier on her shoulder, and this would lighten the load.

"Now, don't eat it all," she warned, "We'll need food for dinner."

Wally looked about in dismay. Too late.

"Oh, well," smiled Sarah, "at least we won't have to carry anything heavy anymore!"

The sun was high in the sky now and it was very warm. Butterflies fluttered and bees droned among the flowers and grass, and it was soft and comfy in the shade of the old log.

"Maybe we could take just a little nap," said Sarah drowsily.

But Wally was already asleep.

Sarah awoke with a start. For a moment she was confused, then spied the remains of their lunch.

"Oh, yes," she remembered, without quite the morning's enthusiasm, "I'm running away from home."

She gathered up the sandwich wrappers and apple cores, and tied the bundles back onto their sticks. She felt dusty and sticky and hot. Why hadn't she brought something to drink?

Wally was awake and rubbing his eyes. Putting his glasses back on, he peered at the sky. The sun was way over on the other side now. They stood up and looked into the distance.

"We haven't been found yet," Sarah said with disappointment. "I don't think anyone is even looking for us."

This confused Wally no end, who thought this was their very purpose.

"Which way should we go, Sarah?"

Sarah thought for a moment.

"Well, we can't keep heading for the river. We might see Mr. or Mrs. Beaver and they'll ask all kinds of questions. Besides, we couldn't get across."

When she visited the Beavers with her mother, they would stand on the bank and wave or call out, and Thad or Franklin or Mr. Beaver would row over and bring them to the other side. No, they couldn't very well do that now.

Anyway, she might see some of the Muskrats, and Sarah

didn't like them very much.

"We could try going through the woods."

"No," said Wally. "Mr. Hedgehog will be working there and he would wonder what we were doing out there all alone. And we'd have to pass the Rabbits' house."

"No, I guess not that way," said Sarah hastily, for she knew that if the Rabbit girls spied them, they would chatter and talk and want them to stay and play.

But by now, Wally was getting a little homesick. He yearned for his own backyard and his bedroom with all his own things, and the comfort brought by the familiar and secure.

He brightened.

"I know! Maybe we could just sneak back home for a moment to see what everyone's doing!"

"And get some more food," he added as an after-thought.

"Oh, that's a good idea, Wally! They've probably missed us by now!"

And were probably very upset.

This last thought cheered Sarah somewhat.

But no one appeared to be home as they approached her back wall. Slipping through the gate, they tiptoed alongside the vegetable garden.

Where were they all? wondered Sarah. Could everyone be out looking for them? Wouldn't Mother, at least, stay home in case she turned up safe and sound?

Concentrating on the house and the whereabouts of her family, Sarah and Wally were startled to hear a voice.

"So there you are! You were both up and out early."

Sarah looked around and saw her next door neighbor, Mrs. Mole, hanging out her washing on the line. Sarah smiled weakly.

"Hello, Mrs. Mole."

"Mama!" said Wally.

Mrs. Mole eyed the two rumpled and still sleepy-eyed children.

"I'm almost finished here. Do you two want to come in and have some lunch and cold lemonade?"

Yes! Oh, yes!

They both rushed into the house to wash up and were seated at the table with shining faces and clean hands when Mrs. Mole came in.

Dishing up their plates, from which Sarah and Wally could not remove their gaze, she said, "So, you both start to school next week?"

"Yes," answered Sarah politely, still keeping one eye on the food, "Wally and Roberta and me."

"Maybe you're not all that excited about it?" inquired Mrs. Mole.

Sarah looked over at Wally. She saw his anxiety as he waited for her answer. She still wasn't so sure about school, but she was sure of one thing. She wasn't going to get Wally in trouble for running away with her.

"Well, at first I wasn't. But maybe it won't be so bad."

Wally smiled at her in relief.

Sarah smiled back.

After all, what were friends for?

Sarah was home in time for dinner.

No one said anything about her absence, but chattered on about inconsequential things until Roscoe mentioned school.

They all grew quiet and Roscoe glanced at her sideways.

Sarah smiled and gazed back at him. She had not needed to follow Roscoe to have an adventure. She and Wally had had one of their own.

And maybe, after all, that's what school would be -- another Great Adventure.

# III - School Daze

Sarah and Roberta were usually awakened by the sun shining cheerily through their window, but on this first day of school, Sarah was up in the dim gray light of early morning. She had made her bed and straightened her side of the room. She had washed her face and brushed her teeth and dressed. And now she was placing things one by one into her backpack.

Roberta was still huddled beneath the covers.

Mother Mouse peeked in the room. "What are you doing, Sarah?" she asked curiously.

"Just some things I need, Mother," replied Sarah firmly,

continuing to place the items neatly in the pack.

Mother leaned over slightly to see, then went on downstairs.

"She's packing enough to feed an army," thought Mother. "Why does she think she'll need all that food?"

But Sarah knew. Today was the beginning of her great adventure. But as her misgivings grew about exactly what kind of adventure this would turn out to be, she thought of her provisions as treats, little presents for herself, to help her get through a day which might not turn out exactly as she expected.

The sun was coming through the dining room window when Sarah came down to the table for breakfast.

By now the others were also downstairs and Mother was dishing out the hot oatmeal. Sarah watched Roscoe put butter and maple sugar in his, then looked at Sam, who swirled his with honey. She slowly poured her favorites, sugar and cream, into her oatmeal and mechanically began to eat. But this morning it didn't seem to have much taste at all. She couldn't even finish it, because it just lay heavily in her stomach.

Mother helped them put on boots, jackets, hats, and scarves which she had warmed at the fireplace, for in spite of the sun, the mornings were cold.

Sarah struggled with her backpack. Her eyes and little pink nose could barely be seen between her hat and scarf, hand-me-downs from Sam, and her new jacket, bought for her "to grow into."

With a hug and a pat, and a sigh of relief, Mother sent them out the door and off to school.

Sarah trudged down the road with the others, but heard and saw no one, so absorbed was she in her own misery. Roberta and her brothers called out to their friends as each joined the stream of excited children headed for school. They laughed, they chattered, they scattered the red and gold leaves and called to stragglers running to catch up.

All but Sarah.

Little Megan Squirrel walked alongside her for a short distance, prattling cheerily to the silent, muffled figure. Megan finally grew silent herself and rushed off to join another group of children.

Sarah even rebuffed Wally's overtures of friendliness. After all, if it hadn't been for him, she would have been gone far, far away, and would never have had to face this ordeal.

Her only comfort was the food in her backpack, nearly crowding out her tablet and pencils.

She lagged behind the others as they took the path up a small rise and descended into the schoolyard. Ahead of her through the trees, she could see a white building topped with a red tower. In the tower was a bell and its ringing tones seemed to Sarah to be saying "Hur-ry! Hur-ry!"

This only increased her anxiety.

Still trailing her friends, Sarah finally climbed the school's wide stairs. There stood Mrs. Givens. Pointy-nosed, with spectacles over her small, close-set eyes, but beaming at the children with a kind face and smile, the teacher greeted each by name. When Roberta and Sarah arrived, Mrs. Givens pointed out the cloakroom and then showed them their seats -- thankfully, thought Sarah, right next to each other.

If she somehow made a fool of herself, she could hope that only Roberta would notice and that (maybe) Roberta would be discreet about it.

The chattering, the rustling, the scraping of desks quieted as Mrs. Givens called the class to order.

Sarah's stomach was still in a knot. What had she thought bringing all that food was going to do? She doubted she would be able to eat any of it.

What were Mother and Skitch doing now? Who would watch Skitch for her while she cleaned up the dishes? Who would sweep out the kitchen and the back porch? A wave of homesickness swept over her.

Mrs. Givens' voice came through Sarah's musings. What was she talking about?

Homework, school rules.

Sarah panicked for a moment. She hadn't heard any of it. What if she broke one of the rules she didn't even know about? What had Mrs. Givens said about homework?

"Now, I'm going to pass out paper," said Mrs. Givens, beginning to walk up and down the aisles, "and there are crayons and colored pencils in your desk. I want each of you to draw a picture of what you did that you liked best this past summer. But for you older children," she added, looking to the back of the room where Roscoe and his classmates sat, "I want you to write a short composition."

There were groans, of course. Robbie Hedgehog looked longingly at the crayons as he returned them to his desk and pulled out his pencil instead.

For 10 or 15 minutes there was silence in the room, save for the scratching of pencils on paper, a few whispers and giggles, and the slight occasional squeak of chalk as Mrs. Givens wrote on the blackboard.

Sarah glanced up. Mrs. Givens was putting her name and the school hours on the board. Thank goodness it was in printed letters and not handwriting.

Sarah returned to her picture. She had quickly reviewed all the things she had done this summer -- helping Mother in the house; playing with Skitch; playing house with her friends the Rabbit sisters under the hydrangea bushes; visiting the Beavers with her mother. She remembered being rowed across the river in Mr. Beaver's boat, and playing in the meadow with Megan Squirrel.

She finally settled on an elaborate picture in two parts: one side showed Mother and Sarah in the kitchen, fixing sandwiches and pies and packing them in a large basket. The other side showed them all -- Mother, Sarah, Skitch, Roberta, Sam and Roscoe -- walking out to the meadow on their picnic. It all seemed to have happened such a long time ago!

By the time Mrs. Givens collected the drawings and

compositions and resumed her talk to the class about the work they would be doing that school year, Sarah had begun to relax.

The sun was beaming through the classroom windows, and the room seemed warmer and friendlier.

But then she froze. What was it that Mrs. Givens had just said?

"Now, for the benefit of our new students this year, I want each of you in turn to stand, face the class and introduce yourself."

Sarah glanced around furtively.

She would be the last one. Seated as she was in the front of the room, she would have to stand and turn around to a sea of faces.

The fact that she knew them all, and that most were her friends, made no difference whatsoever.

How she wished that she and Wally had just kept on walking that day! They could have been way, far away, across the river, someplace where there was no school!

There was a roaring in Sarah's head, which was becoming so loud she could scarcely hear the introductions. Each child seemed more clever and witty in turn. Sarah wondered what her voice would sound like.

A frog, probably.

Would her face turn red, as it often did when she was nervous or embarrassed? And she was so shy! A chatterbox at home, Sarah was quieter outside of her family circle. When she went with her mother to visit the Beavers, or the Squirrel family, or Mrs. Hedgehog, she had to be reminded by Mother to say hello, and even then it came out in a near whisper. But Mother was always there, and that had made it bearable.

Sarah suddenly remembered Mrs. Mole's words to her one day when talking about her shyness. "Now, remember, Sarah, those who are shy are just a little too taken up with themselves. And that's sad, isn't it? Because then there is no room to be interested in others."

This had made Sarah wish desperately to be more like Roberta, for now she felt that she not only bore the stigma of shyness, but of selfishness as well. But no matter how hard she tried, nothing seemed to change things.

And then it was Sarah's turn.

It felt as if all the eyes in the room were boring holes in her back. Beads of perspiration lined her brow and her gray fur looked clumped and dark.

She started to rise, but stumbled and fell back suddenly into her seat.

"Yowww!" she exclaimed.

She heard smothered giggles. What had happened?

Looking down at her feet, Sarah realized she had tripped over the straps of her backpack on the floor beside her desk.

She had bumped her elbow on the desk when she

tripped, too, but hardly felt the pain in her embarrassment. She felt a hand support her and looked up with tears in her eyes at Mrs. Givens.

But Sarah was determined to continue. She turned to face the class. Her elbow started to hurt. There were more giggles and Sarah leaned slightly against her desk to help support her wobbly legs.

"Eek!" Sarah squeaked and brushed at her eyes in panic.

It was only the end of her hair ribbon, which had come undone and now flopped in front of her face. Her classmates were laughing hysterically.

In her utter misery, Sarah could not see Wally's sympathetic face or hear Mrs. Givens shushing the class. She glanced at Roberta for support, but was met with betrayal.

Roberta had her hands over her mouth to hold in the laughter. When she saw Sarah's mournful face, Roberta stifled a whoop and put her head down to her desk, unable to hold it in any longer.

Still gazing fixedly at Roberta, Sarah spoke.

"M-M-My name is Roberta."

The raucous laughter again burst forth around her.

Tears were brimming in Sarah's eyes and her ears were tingling. This was all just a bad dream -- it had to be. She hurriedly picked up her backpack, cramming the spilled articles in any which way, then scampered to the cloakroom by the front door.

She would just get her things and put them on, she thought, buttoning her coat and beginning to wrap the wool scarf around her neck.

"Sarah?"

She turned to see Mrs. Givens at the doorway. Sarah finished wrapping her scarf, then placed the fuzzy hat on her head and picked up her backpack.

*...But Sarah was determined to continue.*

"I'm going home," she said in a wavering voice, "and

I'm not coming back."

Mrs. Givens hesitated a moment as Sarah marched out the door, then passed back into the classroom and motioned Roscoe to her desk.

Sarah continued on her solitary way towards home.

Well, some adventure this turned out to be, she thought. She had known all along that it was going to be a disaster. She didn't want to go to school, and she was not going to go to school, and that was that.

Sarah's walk slowed as she came closer to home. She would have to tell Mother, of course. But Mother would understand.

Mother had better understand, she thought rebelliously.

Muttering to herself, Sarah walked in the front door of her house. Mother Mouse, startled at seeing Sarah back so soon, rushed towards her.

"Sarah! What's wrong? Why are you home from school?"

She felt the warmth enclose her when she entered her old familiar surroundings, and at the sight of Mother's face, loving and concerned, tears welled up again in Sarah's eyes.

"Oh, Mother," she cried, dropping her backpack and running to the beloved figure, "It was awful!"

Then Mother took Sarah in her lap and they sat together in the big rocking chair. Sarah told her everything, sobbed a little, and interspersed her story with comments about stupid backpacks and dumb hair ribbons and mean children.

Mother rocked her gently and let her ramble on. Finally Sarah realized that Mother had not responded to all of the terrible things that had happened and sat up.

"It was really awful, Mother! I'm not going back, I'm going to stay here and help you in the house, and keep it clean, and bake pies, and take care of Skitch, just like we used to do."

But Mother was silent and thoughtful.

"Don't you want me here, Mother?" Sarah faltered.

Mother's smile was quick.

"Of course I would love to have you here with me, Sarah…"

"But what, Mother?" Would Mother make her go back there? Sarah shuddered.

"It's just that I want so much more for you, Sarah."

Slipping her daughter from her lap, Mother led Sarah down the hall. They paused at the door of Father's library.

Sarah's tears stopped.

Father's library had always been his very private area, off limits to the children except for special occasions. This was where he had worked and read and studied.

Mother opened the door and Sarah was overwhelmed with memories of her father.

There were the walls of books reaching to the ceiling, the big dark wooden desk in the center of the room, the glorious paintings on the wall. Sarah remembered the feel of the soft rug beneath her feet.

Since their father's death, the children had not been in the room. Mother kept it clean and dusted and sometimes went in to sit for a few quiet moments. The door was not locked. Mother trusted her children's sense of honor and respect for her wishes, so they passed the door each day without a thought of entering, only with a comforting feeling that Father's library and his things were safe inside.

This, thought Sarah, made it feel as if something of him were still with them. Sometimes she had even imagined a little that if she did open the door one day, there he would be, sitting in the big chair at his desk, books piled up and opened before him, the smoke from his pipe circling above him and drifting out the window that overlooked the side garden.

"Your father loved learning," mused Mother, and Sarah listened intently. "He loved it almost as much as he loved all of you."

Mother smiled -- a happy smile, noted Sarah.

"He wanted you to learn as much as you could throughout your life, and he knew that school was just the beginning."

Mother turned to look down at Sarah.

"What the other children think or say of you is not important. I know, I know," she forestalled Sarah's protest,

"It seems important now, and I know that it hurt when they laughed at you. But this will pass in time."

No, thought Sarah, Mother's wrong. I won't ever forget it.

At the look on Sarah's face, Mother sighed.

"Do you remember when you fell off your bike and didn't want to ride it anymore? You were going to give it away."

Sarah smiled in spite of herself. She remembered how angry she had been at the "stupid old bike" that had run her into the hedge. She had planned to give it to Cassie Rabbit -- that is, until she saw Cassie mount it and ride effortlessly down the road, turn and swoop back to Sarah with laughing eyes. She had thought then, why, it looks like fun!

"Now," continued Mother, "you don't think anything of getting on that bike and riding into the village. It was hard at first, but now it's just part of the many things you do, and it makes a lot of them easier. It's a useful skill, and you'll never forget how to use it."

Sarah thought for a moment.

"You mean there's things I'll learn at school that will make other things easier to do? Like going to the village store on errands is quicker with my bike?"

"Yes, Sarah, and more. Learning is something that we all do naturally in life. You all learned to walk and talk and do the things to help me around the house. Now there's learning of another kind, and the best way to get it..."

"Is to go to school," said Sarah despondently.

Sarah walked over to Father's desk and gently placed her hand on the books lying there.

A sudden noise made both Sarah and Mother turn to the doorway. Roscoe stood there, breathless and windblown, a note in his hand.

"Mrs. Givens sent me home with this, to make sure that Sarah was all right," he said, glancing with both anxiety and curiosity at Sarah.

"Sarah's fine, Roscoe, and I'll just write a little note to Mrs. Givens to let her know that Sarah will be back tomorrow," Mother responded, drawing a reluctant Roscoe from the room and closing the library door, leaving Sarah alone inside.

Sarah pulled herself up into father's chair and snuggled into it.

She could almost feel his arm around her, the soft shiny cloth of his waistcoat against her cheek, the way he would smooth her fur back from her forehead when he sat and read to her.

"What's the problem, Sarah Mouse?" he would have said.

And then she would have told him everything: all about school, about Mrs. Givens, about her ordeal, about how Roberta had acted, even about running away.

They would have sat in silence for a moment.

"So you tripped over your backpack."

"Yes." Frowning.

"Then your ribbons fell over your face?"

"Yes." Scowling.

"And then -- and then -- you told all of your friends who have known you, for goodness sakes, for years -- that your name was Roberta?"

"Yes." Puzzled.

Father chuckled.

Sarah was astounded.

Would Father have laughed at her, too?

"I think," said Father gently, "that I might have been tempted -- just a little bit! -- to laugh, too, Sarah. Oh, I know it wouldn't have been the kind thing to do, but after all, what you told me was funny, you know! And laughter is such a happy thing!"

Sarah sat stormily silent.

Funny! Happy!

Well, maybe it was a little funny -- especially if you thought of it all happening to someone else. What if it had been Megan Squirrel who ran away from home all day and no one noticed? Or who put so much food in her backpack she could hardly carry it to school? Or Patty Possum up there telling everyone her name was Roberta?

She laughed out loud.

The image of self-possessed Patty standing in front of the class with her hair ribbon dangling in her face, her feet in her backpack straps and saying, "I'm Roberta!" tickled Sarah's funny bone.

Sarah slipped from the chair. She looked around the room once more, then back at Father's chair.

"It wasn't nice of them to laugh," she whispered.

"No-o-o, not nice," came Father's voice softly, "but after all…"

"I know," grinned Sarah, "it was funny!"

Sarah stood still in the center of the room, amazed at how she felt so enfolded, so -- so -- secure in love and memories of her father. Then she walked to the door. Placing her hand on the doorknob, she whispered, "Good-bye, Daddy," and walked into the hall.

Roscoe was just leaving with his mother's note in his hand. He stopped.

"Why were you in Father's library, Sarah?" he whispered.

"I was just having a talk with Daddy," she said serenely as she stepped past him, leaving Roscoe round-eyed with wonder.

# IV - Sam's Stuff

"Well, Sarah," sighed Mother Mouse, "I can't put it off any longer. Thank you so much for helping me."

Mother was uncomfortable because she had long postponed a most unpleasant task. So, before she could become disheartened by pondering the work ahead of her, she moved quickly about the house in preparation.

Thus, on a bright and beautiful autumn morning, Mother and Sarah, armed with broom and mop, dust cloth and disinfectant, climbed the stairs to Sam's room.

They paused in the doorway, momentarily taken aback.

"It's sort of messy, isn't it?" said Sarah in a small voice.

Mother felt weary already, but squared her shoulders and entered the room.

"I know he will not clean his room really well by himself. It's just not going to happen. So maybe we can get him off to a good start. If you'll pick up his toys and books, Sarah, I'll gather his clothes for the laundry."

As Sarah began dusting the shelves and collecting the assortment of items that should have sat upon them, Mother picked up socks and shirts.

"Where is the other one?" she muttered, looking around her with a blue sock in one hand and trousers and shirt clutched in another.

"Here's his tie -- he said he'd lost it somewhere! And here's Roscoe's green shirt -- no wonder he couldn't find it!"

Mother Mouse removed it from the desk where, rolled into a tight little ball, it had been used to prop up an empty bird's nest.

"These curtains will have to come down and be washed," said Mother, "and all the bedding taken off as well."

While Mother surveyed the room again for any odd clothing that might be lurking in a corner, Sarah was down on her tummy, scooting under the bed to retrieve anything she might find.

Suddenly she shrieked.

Her fur laced with cobwebs and dust, Sarah skittered out from under the bed, jumped up, and was out of the room in a flash. Mother's eyes followed her in bewilderment.

Hovering outside the door, Sarah exclaimed, "There's something -- ahchoo! ahchoo! -There's something under there! I felt it! It -- it -- wriggled!

Mother Mouse had already spied the small garden snake, which looked almost as alarmed as Sarah, slithering from under the quilt. She reached for a jar -- there were plenty around the room -- tilted it onto its side and laid it down on the floor. The snake quickly slid in and Mother placed a book on top of the jar and set it carefully on the dresser.

"Mother, I just can't go back in there!" wailed Sarah, wringing her hands and peering around the door.

"That's all right, Sarah," replied Mother in a distracted manner, one eye on the jar. "Just go on downstairs and I'll finish up -- you were such a big help, I'll be done in no time now."

Still apologizing and now and then giving a little shudder, Sarah made her way downstairs to comb her fur and bemoan the streaks of dust and dirt on her dress.

Meanwhile, Mother Mouse resumed cleaning with a vengeance.

She swept the floor and even the walls and ceiling, brushing down a confusion of cobwebs and spiders. She mopped and scrubbed and polished, and assembled a bewildering jumble of objects that she piled with increasing vexation on Sam's bed. Whatever she could identify, she placed where it belonged -- books in the bookcase, toys on the shelves or in the old wooden chest. She grouped together on a little table those items that might (with some stretch of the imagination) be considered part of a nature collection, but many were unidentifiable or were moldy with age. There were things she hesitated to touch at all, but eventually lifted gingerly with thumb and fingertip and placed in a large basket to be taken downstairs and, yes, definitely, thought Mother Mouse, outside.

Throughout all these ministrations to Sam's room, Sarah could hear from below Mother's mutterings and mumblings and, now and then, a squeak of alarm.

None of this augured well for Sam.

When Sam sauntered in the door that afternoon, it was with a light heart. But he stopped abruptly as the short fur on his back quivered.

Something was wrong.

He glanced first at his mother who was in her chair, eyes steadfastly on the mending in her lap, then to Sarah, who returned his gaze with -- what? -- resentment?

He eased towards the stairs, then halted when he heard his mother's voice.

"Sam, come here, please."

His shoulders slumped. From the tone of her voice he knew it meant trouble, and he walked wearily back into the living room.

Had she found out about the book he had left out in the rain, its pages now swollen to twice their thickness and the print illegible?

Had Roberta told on him when she found him in the sycamore tree hunkered down over the bird nest with the baby birds in it, while the mother screeched and swooped in and out among the leaves? He had only wanted to see them.

He stood before his mother with anxious eyes.

"I cleaned out your room today, Sam," said Mother.

Sam became wary.

"I want it kept the way it is right now. I don't ever want to see it in that condition again."

Sam nodded and turned to go, stopping as his mother spoke again.

"And Sam, there's a basket of things from your room in the backyard. I want you to go through them, and pick out three things you want to keep. But before you take them back upstairs, you are to show them to me for my approval."

Sam's shoulders slumped even further.

"And one more thing," went on Mother.

It took every bit of strength Sam had to turn around. What now?

"There is to be nothing -- nothing -- well, nothing live kept in your room. Do you understand?"

Sam straightened immediately and, looking from

Mother to Sarah, demanded, "What did you do with my snake?"

"We turned it loose in the field, Sam," replied his mother. "It is not a kind thing to do, to keep a wild creature boxed in like that."

"Or to keep it in the house with us,' added Sarah feelingly.

"He liked me," declared Sam, "I fed him and everything."

"I'm sure you thought you were taking good care of it," soothed his mother, "but it still stands that you are not to bring indoors any creatures -"

She paused for a moment, aware of her son's tendency to translate literally what she said, wondering what he might be able to come up with which was not covered by the word "creature." Then she continued:

"Nothing living."

Sam stood and pondered for a moment.

"What about leaves and flowers?" he inquired.

"Leaves and flowers -- botanical specimens -- are all right," said Mother. "Within reason," she added hastily, recalling some of the things removed from Sam's room.

"What about food?" he asked.

"No food."

Sam thought a moment more.

"What about furniture and paper, and books? They were alive once -- they were trees and bark, and the book covers -"

*"Sam, there's a basket of things from your room in the backyard. I want you to go through them, and pick out three things you want to keep."*

His voice faltered at the look in his mother's eyes, and he realized that she was quickly reaching the limits of her patience.

"Okay, okay, I was just joking," he mumbled feebly.

"Well, it was no joke to Sarah and me when we cleaned that room today," retorted Mother. "Now go on and put your things away, then come back down and sort the basket out."

Sam walked heavily up the stairs. He opened the door to his room and glanced around with leaden eye. Just as he suspected, they had taken out all his good stuff. He sat down at his desk, giving it a cursory look as he did so.

Well, it would probably be easier to work at with all the stuff cleared off it.

He sighed and looked around.

Why, there was his baseball, sitting on the shelf over his bed! He thought Robbie Hedgehog had taken it the last time they played in the empty field.

He opened his desk drawer. There were all the pencils and pens and rulers and whatnot arranged in separate sections, neat and handy.

Sam gazed into space.

Maybe this wouldn't be so bad after all.

Late that night, as Mother Mouse climbed the stairs, she noticed light coming from Sam's room. Tapping softly at his door, but receiving no answer, she opened it slightly. At the sight of Sam sprawled in his bed, she entered to cover him up and turn out the light. Spread out around him were tablet and pencil and she picked them up to place them on his desk.

Her eye caught the first line in his odd little back-slanted writing: "My Stuff."

It's one of his poems, Mother realized, and began to put it away. But she couldn't resist reading just a few lines, and of course, then, the whole thing.

MY STUFF
by Sam

Mom said "your room is a mess" and "enough!"
And made me clean out all my valuable stuff.

So there it all sits in a pitiful pile,
"Three things you can keep" said my mom with a smile.

I sat down to sort all my valuable stuff.
How can she think that three things are enough?

These rocks that I kept (well, sometimes) in a drawer
They're petrified teeth from an old dinosaur!

This flashlight would work, it just needs a spring…
And batteries, a bulb….And this other thing,

Not sure what it is, but it's made of real metal.
My jar full of mud -- shake it up, let it settle –

The water is clear -- you can drink it (I've tried),
My insect collection (well, they have kind of dried).

My real diamond ring (well, the diamond is lost)
But if it were there, who'd know what it cost!

Why, looking at all of this valuable stuff,
How can she think that three things are enough?

When she was finished, Mother Mouse laid the tablet gently on the desk, then turned again to Sam. Seeing his face peaceful in sleep and recalling his agonizing decisions over what things to keep and what to part with, her heart softened at the thought of his distress.

Smiling again at the image of Sam consoling himself with his "literary effusions", she smoothed the fur on his forehead and pulled the quilt up to tuck it beneath his chin.

Perhaps she had been a little harsh on him.

The room had been a mess, though, she reminded herself.

Turning to leave the room, she stumbled, only preventing a fall by catching herself on the nightstand. Sam continued to snore gently. She regained her balance and then looked down to see her feet entangled in a small pile of clothing -- Sam's pants and shirt.

She could only see one sock. Mother Mouse sighed.

# *V - HALLOWE'EN SCARES*

The golden haze of autumn sunlight had given way to frosty mornings. The town awakened sleepily to begin its day at sunrise. Leisurely walks, children's play, and neighborly conversations in the warm twilights were drawing to a close, and lamps were lit earlier in the evening. Each night smoke rose from chimneys into the cool dark air, and a silver moon glittered in a star-filled sky.

A last revel remained before winter arrived -- it was only a few days until Hallowe'en.

"It was a dark and stormy night..."

In a hoarse whisper, Sam began his story. Seated on a low stool by the fireplace, he faced the three excited listeners huddled together in Mother's big, overstuffed chair: Roberta, who wore a little air of condescension; Sarah, already shivery in anticipation; and Skitch, who understood not one word in five, but picked up cues on how to behave and react from his sisters.

"There was a monster loose in the town and no one had been able to catch him. No one ever saw him, either, only a large hulking shadow in the moonlight."

Sam paused, then continued, his voice sinking even deeper.

"Already six people had been strangled in the night..."

Sarah squeaked and covered her eyes. Skitch did likewise, peering out almost immediately from behind one paw to make sure that he was not missing out on something.

Sam resumed his tale.

"The town lived in terror! Who would be next? It could be anyone! The monster climbed into windows and attacked little children in their beds, or snuck up behind them in the dark! It was Hallowe'en night and the children could not go out Trick or Treating, because the monster was sure to be on the prowl!"

Sarah gave a little moan, echoed by Skitch.

In the kitchen, Mother Mouse was working in cheerful ignorance of the terror being created in the small group clustered around the hearth.

Sam continued his tale:

"The police told everyone not to have lights in their houses, so that the monster couldn't sneak up to a window and see everyone inside. People locked their doors and windows and some were even afraid to light fires in their fireplaces. They huddled in their houses, terrified, and would scream when the wind blew leaves against a window, or a shutter banged against a wall."

They all started when the wind outside gave a low moan and something clattered in the garden.

*Even Roberta was uneasy now, shifting in the chair so that no arm or leg was outside of its comforting protection.*

Even Roberta was uneasy now, shifting in the chair so

that no arm or leg was outside of its comforting protection.

Sarah's eyes, unblinking, darted among the shadows thrown on the walls by the dying fire. Skitch looked around, too. He was beginning to feel a little depressed -- he had thought there would be more action and noise and laughter, and maybe something good to eat. But here he sat, wedged in between his two sisters, listening to his brother who was, well, scary, so different from the Sam who played with him and tickled him during the daytime.

Sam was uneasy, too, but for quite a different reason. If Mother knew what he was doing...!

What had Roscoe gotten him into? Sam felt tricked -- making a promise to do whatever Roscoe wanted, all in exchange for a dumb cat's eye marble from Mr. Possum's store!

He suspected that Roscoe was up to no good. And he was about to come to the worst part of the story.

With a worried glance towards the kitchen, but resigned to finishing the tale, Sam pitched his voice even lower, and the hoarse, gravelly tones that emerged froze Sarah into immobility and struck terror in Skitch's little heart.

"One house sat away from the town, by itself in a field. The father was away and there was only the mother and her five children."

"Like us!" whispered Sarah.

"They had done everything they could -- locked and bolted the doors, turned off all the lights, and all of them sat bunched together around a cold, dead fireplace, moonlight streaming in from the window behind them."

"Is this about our house?" gasped Roberta.

Sarah uttered a small whimper.

"Suddenly," continued Sam, leaning closer to the group, "they heard a noise! Was it the wind? A tree branch? Or -- ?

"Gradually the moonlight was blocked out. Turning slowly to the window, they saw a large hulking shape..."

Sam's story was suddenly interrupted by shrieks from Roberta and Sarah! Something cold had wisped past their shoulders! They jumped up and ran into the kitchen, screaming at the top of their lungs.

Sam was horrified at the ruckus, and quickly scooped up Skitch, who had begun to cry loudly. Roscoe came from behind the chair, holding up two clammy rubber gloves and shaking with laughter. Sam glowered at him reproachfully while trying unsuccessfully to silence Skitch.

"It was the monster -- I felt its hands touch me!" wailed Sarah from the kitchen.

"Well, we're in for it now," muttered Sam.

He could hear his mother's soft murmur and Sarah's wail tapering off into a gentle sobbing. Conscience-stricken, he continued to bounce Skitch on his knee. Baby had stopped crying and, glad to have the brother he knew back, kept patting Sam's face.

Roscoe, too, realized they were in for it.

At first it had seemed like a good trick on his sisters -- and on Sam as well. But now it didn't seem like such a good idea after all.

Roscoe sat down near the hearth just as the kitchen door opened.

A large hulking shadow, backlit in the nearly darkened room by the kitchen light, loomed menacingly before them: it was Mother, with Sarah and Roberta clinging to her skirts.

* * * * *

Roscoe awakened the next morning in a cheerful mood. The events of the evening before were already receding into the dim mists of the past.

Of course, Mother had had some pretty hard words for him and Sam, and Sarah and Roberta had gotten to stay up and eat the caramel apples that Mother had made. He and Sam had had to go to bed, and -- oh, yes -- Sam was not talking to him, "anymore, ever."

Roscoe knew Sam would get over it, for Sam seldom held grudges.

The only good part was when Mother had turned to Sarah and Roberta and exclaimed, "And whatever possessed you to sit there with Skitch -- with little Skitch! -- and listen to that story?!"

Sarah had been stricken and penitent, but Roberta smoldered. Roscoe knew that even her look of self-satisfied triumph when he and Sam were sent to bed would not be enough.

Roberta would want revenge.

Roscoe grinned. He was looking forward to it! Let her try her best!

He began to descend the stairs for breakfast, but suddenly stopped, alert to the sound of Sarah's and Roberta's voices from the dining room.

"We'll tell everyone that no one would dare go into the woods on Hallowe'en because of the spirit that haunts them!" said Roberta, "And that will guarantee Roscoe will do it!"

"I know. Think of how everyone will laugh at Roscoe when he comes running out of the woods screaming! You know Roscoe's going to brag at school about how scared we were last night. This would sort of -- of..."

"Save our reputations?"

"Yes, that's it."

Sarah and Roberta giggled, pleased with themselves.

Roscoe remained hunkered down by the railing. Spirit? What spirit? He'd never heard anything about the woods being haunted. He slowly realized that this was somehow going to be their feeble attempt at revenge!

"Okay, then, we have our plan," said Roberta. "We'll set it up for Hallowe'en night. You know we'll have to bring Skitch home early from Trick or Treating, then we can meet everyone at the old gate at the edge of the woods."

Roscoe's leg was in a cramp, but he made himself stay there while the girls finished breakfast and took their bowls to the kitchen. Straining to hear more as they gathered their books together, he was startled by a noise behind him. He turned his head to see Sam come out of his room, look curiously at him and continue, silent and stiff, down the stairs.

Roscoe breathed a sigh of relief, glad for the moment that Sam was not speaking to him. Well, at least now he could go downstairs, he thought, hearing the bang of the front door as Sarah and Roberta left for school.

The fact that Sam pointedly ignored him was lost on Roscoe during breakfast.

What was it, exactly, they were plotting, he wondered, reviewing the overheard conversation. It was probably all Roberta's idea -- it seemed like one of her crackpot schemes. Contemplating all of this, Roscoe gazed past Sam and through the dining room window. It was filled with light this morning and he could see the sycamore tree, and the old wall with the forlorn branches of the rose clambering over it.

Something was missing.

The curtains. The sheer white curtains that usually covered the window and filtered the morning light.

Mother must be doing laundry today, he thought absently.

A smile played over his face as his mind wandered from Sarah and Roberta to thoughts of Hallowe'en night, his costume which he was planning to buy in Mr. Possum's store, and all the fun he was going to have. He pondered again the overheard conversation, trying to figure out their "plan."

Sam, sneaking a look, was vaguely irritated that his "cold treatment" was not having more of an impact on Roscoe.

Mother Mouse was just walking into the dining room with Sam's and Roscoe's lunches as Roscoe was rushing out the door.

It had suddenly come to him why the curtains were missing!

"Why did Roscoe leave without his lunch?" asked Mother, bewildered.

Sam shrugged.

"Well, you'll just have to take it with you and give it to him at school."

Sam shrugged again. Now he could finish eating breakfast in peace.

Roscoe continued making his Hallowe'en plans on the way to school. No more clown and hobo and ghost costumes for him! This year he would really look great, he thought joyfully.

When he arrived at the schoolyard, he looked around

until he saw Hiram Hedgehog and Thaddeus Beaver, and then went up and joined them.

"Have you heard the little kids saying anything about a ghost in the woods?" he asked.

Thaddeus looked puzzled, but Hiram laughed.

"A ghost in the woods! This must be some Hallowe'en stuff they've come up with. Dad and Homer are in the woods all day long, year 'round, and I never heard anything like that!"

"Maybe Robbie knows about it," said Roscoe, looking around for Homer's youngest brother.

"Why don't you ask your sisters?" inquired Thad.

Roscoe grinned. "Well, they were talking about it this morning -- about Hallowe'en night and the 'spirit that haunts the woods'!"

"Hey, there's Robbie," said Thad. "Robbie! Come over here a minute!"

"Have you heard anything about a ghost in the woods?" asked Hiram.

"Yeah! You didn't know about it? It only walks on Hallowe'en night, and it can't go outside of the woods," responded Robbie. "It goes after anyone who comes in," he added in a confidential tone.

"Where did you get that idea from?" asked Hiram curiously.

"Roberta told me all about it."

"Well," joked Thad, "I guess now you know!"

He and Hiram wandered off towards the school steps, leaving a smug Roscoe still looking after Robbie.

Roberta had told him, had she? So they were spreading the word to the other children!

"Patty!" he called as she passed by.

"What, Roscoe?"

"Have you heard anything about the woods being haunted..."

"Yes, oh, yes! Sarah told me she thinks it's someone who used to live in the old mansion -- that maybe they killed someone and can't rest!"

She shivered.

"Isn't it fun! But scary!"

Roscoe wandered around the schoolyard while he waited for the bell to ring.

He questioned Annie and Betty Rabbit, who shuffled and giggled, but confirmed that, yes, Sarah and Roberta had told them about the ghost in the woods on Hallowe'en night. Molly Beaver knew about it as well.

Roscoe spent the morning making feverish plans. Mrs. Givens' voice droned in the background, something about fractions and common denominators.

The noon bell interrupted his thoughts and he realized class was over. Everyone was getting lunch and going outside, chattering about their Hallowe'en activities, about costumes, about which house gave out the best Hallowe'en treats.

Roscoe ran outside, positioning himself where he could make his announcement.

Make his announcement, that is, without letting Sarah and Roberta know that he was aware that this, too, was all part of their "plan."

He knew they were counting on him to rise to the challenge and go into the haunted woods, brave soul that he was!

So when Roscoe told his schoolmates that he, Roscoe Mouse, would be confronting the "spirit" on Hallowe'en night, their oohs and aahs of admiration meant less to him than the sight of Sarah and Roberta exchanging delighted grins.

Let them laugh now, he thought.

They won't be laughing when they come hopping through the woods wearing the dining room curtains!

# *VI - Hallowe'en II: Revenge*

"There's a full moon tonight, so that should help, but I want you to hold tightly to Skitch's hand," mumbled Mother Mouse to Sarah and Roberta, her mouth full of straight pins. They remained respectfully silent, but they had already heard this several times in the last few days. Their thoughts were elsewhere.

"Turn, Sarah."

Sarah turned obediently, her arms angled out stiffly

from her sides. She looked down at her costume.

"No, no, no! Don't move!"

Sarah's head bobbed quickly up again.

"There -- all the adjustments are made," sighed Mother, getting up from her knees. She smiled.

"Okay, you can go and look now."

Sarah walked carefully to the large standing mirror in her mother's bedroom and gazed at herself.

"Oh, it's beautiful! I look like a real ballerina!"

Sarah pirouetted. "I'm so glad that Patty grew out of it!"

"Just a few stitches here and there was all it needed," smiled Mother, pleased with the alterations she had made to fit it on Sarah's small frame.

"Can I leave it on until we're ready to go -- please, Mother?" begged Sarah, striking what she imagined was a ballet pose, and almost losing her balance as she glanced over her shoulder to eye herself again in the mirror.

"You can leave on the tights and slippers, but the dress comes off until after dinner," said Mother.

Sarah sighed, and with one last glance at herself in the mirror, slid the billowy tutu over her head.

After all, she thought happily, it's only a few more hours.

She pulled on her school dress, pausing to admire the glistening pink tights and ballet slippers tied with pink ribbon. They gave her such great satisfaction! Her mind on the tutu and how she would look when they went out trick-or-treating -- like a star! -- she started in surprise when Roberta spoke from Mother's bed.

"Oh, stop admiring yourself, Sarah! We've got to tie up the last minute details of our plan!"

Roberta rose from among the soft pillows. Sarah withdrew her thoughts regretfully from contemplation of her own glamour.

"Well, if you'd wanted to be something other than a pumpkin, for goodness sakes, you might be excited, too."

Roberta laughed, taking Sarah by the arm and drawing her up the stairs to their bedroom.

They bounced onto their beds and giggled and plotted and schemed. Their voices were hushed, punctuated with sudden loud "shhh's!," whereupon Roberta would tiptoe to the door, jerk it open, and peer outside to make sure Roscoe could not overhear.

Oblivious to the drama occurring upstairs, Roscoe was washing up for dinner and Mother was placing Skitch in his highchair.

"We have to hurry," said Roscoe to Sam, glancing out the window. "It'll be dark soon."

Sam began to respond, but remembered just in time that he was still not talking to Roscoe.

"There's plenty of time," said Mother comfortingly as she tied a large bib around Skitch's neck.

"But sometimes people run out of the good stuff," recalled Sam a bit anxiously, memories revived of past Hallowe'ens when he had missed out on special treats and had had to settle for dried fruit or old nuts, gathered hastily by some besieged mother for the late stragglers.

Mother laughed.

"You'll get enough of the 'good stuff' to give you a stomach ache for a week!"

At dinner, Mother tried to ignore Roscoe as he bolted his food, and Sam with cheeks stuffed, chewing quickly in a determined effort not to be last. Sarah nibbled at her food and pushed most of it around her plate. Only Skitch behaved normally -- to him it was just another meal.

Roberta seemed deep in thought.

Finally they were dismissed from the table and all flew in different directions to locate and assemble the parts of their costumes.

"Mother!" called Roberta from the upstairs landing, "Did you cut the holes in my pumpkin head?"

"Yes, yes, I just need to make sure they're in the right place -- you'll have to try it on."

"All right, who took my mask?" demanded Sam from his room.

"It's right there on your desk," called Mother, smiling

as she heard the noise and clatter of things being pushed aside.

"Got it!" said Sam breathlessly as he bounded down the stairs. Slipping the mask to his skeleton costume over his face, he snatched up his bag. Mother's voice halted him at the door.

"Wait for Roscoe," she stated firmly.

Muttering under his breath, Sam fidgeted and fumbled in the entry until Roscoe appeared, dressed in a costume that resembled green scales and carrying his mask under his arm.

"Bye!" came two voices at once as the door slammed. Two sets of feet pounded down the path.

"Roscoe didn't even show us his costume," grumbled Roberta as she struggled into her brother's old green Robin Hood tights and jerkin.

"He bought it himself at Mr. Beaver's store," responded Sarah, once again attired in the bouffant pink tutu and lost in self-admiration. "It looked like a lizard or something. What a weird costume!"

By now Roberta was stumbling about the room.

"Mother!" she wailed, her voice echoing in the large hollowed out pumpkin. "I can't see!"

"All right, don't get upset, Roberta! We'll just make the holes a little bigger."

Mother lifted the pumpkin that she had taken from the

garden that morning off of Roberta's shoulders.

Roberta's fur looked mussed and she was nibbling at a pumpkin seed.

*By now Roberta was stumbling about the room. "Mother!" she wailed, her voice echoing in the large hollowed out pumpkin. "I can't see!"*

"It's a good thing Mother made us eat dinner," she giggled, "or I might have ended up eating part of my costume!"

"Um-humh," said Sarah dreamily, practicing a bow in

front of the window where she could see her reflection. Roberta rolled her eyes.

"Just don't get so lost in yourself that you forget our plans."

"Don't worry about that," said Sarah, jolted out of her fantasy.

Mother Mouse returned to the room carrying the pumpkin, Skitch toddling behind her.

"Oh, we've forgotten to get Skitch ready," exclaimed Sarah.

"It will only take a moment," said Mother. "Here, Roberta, try this on again."

"Perfect! I can see perfectly! It's a little heavy, but it sure smells good!"

Skitch gazed in amazement. Why, only a moment before his sister had stood before him, and now it was the giant pumpkin from the garden! With a face! And making sounds! The world was full of miracles!

Mother took advantage of Skitch's temporary transfixion to slip an old tea-cloth over his head, lining up the eye holes she had cut, and pinning it to his clothes so it would not move about.

"Voila!" exclaimed Mother Mouse. "A ghost!"

They all laughed as Skitch, having found the armholes himself, caught sight of his reflection in the window. He touched his face -- so did the thing in the window! As he raised his paw to his head, it did likewise. When Sarah gave the strange thing a bag, Skitch was astonished to find his own chubby paw clutching an identical one. He looked around at everyone and squeaked in excitement.

"Let's go!" grinned Roberta, taking Skitch's paw in one hand and propping up her head with the other.

* * * * *

Later that evening, at the sound of voices and laughter and the quick, light patter of children's footsteps, Mother Mouse emerged from the kitchen where she had just completed what she hoped was her last batch of caramel apples. But before she could reach the door, it swung open and Sarah danced in, eyes aglow, followed by Roberta with Skitch in tow.

Mother leaned down and clucked over Skitch.

"Oh, my poor baby! Roberta, whatever is all this gummy black stuff on him?"

Roberta, glad to be relieved of her charge, handed Skitch over to her mother, who immediately settled into her chair with Skitch on her lap.

"Oh, Mother," exclaimed Sarah, "it was such fun! Everyone loved my costume!"

She continued to flit around the room, still caught up in the excitement of the evening.

"It's licorice," stated Roberta flatly, as Mother unpinned the tea-cloth and carefully drew it off Skitch where it was sticking to his whiskers and mouth. He grinned at his mother, babbling and waving his paws, pointing now to Sarah, now to Roberta.

"Well," laughed Mother, "I guess he's trying to tell me about it!"

"Mrs. Beaver said I looked just like a real ballerina," Sarah said, stopping for a moment to give her mother a quick kiss on the cheek.

"Mrs. Beaver gave Skitch licorice," Roberta added darkly. "He tried to cram it all in his mouth at one time. I don't think he has a single piece of candy left in his bag."

Mother Mouse smiled in amusement at Roberta's air of martyrdom.

"Why didn't you just put it in your own bag?"

"Because he screamed, Mother."

Roberta leaned back in her chair in a weary manner.

"All I did all night was fight with Skitch. Next year," and here she looked at Sarah from under her brows, "someone else can take charge of Skitch while I run around showing off my costume!"

"Well, I told you being a pumpkin was dumb -- and look what happened!" said Sarah. Turning to her mother, Sarah continued her story with such a serious air of drama that Mother hid her smiles by ducking her face behind Skitch's head.

"Mother, I told her to stop taking it off and on -- her old pumpkin head..."

"It was hot and it was heavy," interjected Roberta in her own defense.

"Anyway, she took it off at Mrs. Beaver's..."

"Mrs. Beaver looked at Skitch and said he'd grown, but" (and here Roberta mimicked Mrs. Beaver's feigned concern) "he was looking 'awfully pale'!" A smile flickered across Roberta's face.

"And then," chimed in Sarah, sidetracked for the moment, "Skitch tried to say 'Trick-or-Treat,' didn't he, Roberta? And then he held out his bag. It was so cute!"

Sarah gave Skitch a big hug.

"That's when he got the licorice," said Roberta, looking at her own sticky fingers.

"Well, then Roberta did it again -- took off her head -- at the Moles', and the Hedgehogs', and..."

"All right, Sarah," interrupted Mother Mouse kindly. "I understand, but what finally happened?"

Sarah finished in a rush.

"Mrs. Possum invited us in for pumpkin pie and cider, and Roberta left her head outside on the porch, and Skitch disappeared -- it was just for a moment, Mother -- and we heard this 'munch, munch, munch,' and we found him eating Roberta's pumpkin head! He had already gotten through the eyes and had worked his way to the nose."

Sarah and Mother both looked at Roberta.

"I had to go around the rest of the time dragging Skitch,

and everyone saying, 'oh, how beautiful' and 'what a lovely costume' to Sarah, and 'what a cute little ghost' to Skitch, and then they'd look at me and say, 'and what is your costume, Roberta'? and I'd say, 'I'm a pumpkin…"

Both girls broke into peals of laughter at the memory of the grown-ups' puzzled looks and disconcerted attempts to say something nice about Roberta's costume, which by then lacked its most vital accessory.

"And one little boy," gasped Sarah, "said 'Mommy, she looks more like a green bean'!"

This sent them again into gales of laughter.

"Well," said Mother, wiping her eyes, "why don't we get you all in a nice warm bath…"

"Oh, no, Mother!" cried both girls at once, and Roberta gestured towards the dining room window.

"Oh, that's right," smiled Mother. "Run along then, but don't be too late. And girls," Mother added, her eyes twinkling, "don't be too hard on Roscoe!"

Sarah and Roberta left, chattering excitedly.

"We're probably going to be late," said Sarah, stepping over a tree root on the moonlit path.

"That's okay -- better, probably, because he wouldn't be expecting us to be there, you see?"

"Oh, right," responded Sarah thoughtfully, still pondering the ramifications of their Great Plan.

Roberta, noticing Sarah's furrowed brow, grinned.

"Don't worry, just do what we talked about and practiced and it'll all turn out fine!"

"Look, the kids are all there!"

Several schoolmates turned as Sarah and Roberta approached the group of children clustered around the tall iron gate bordering the entrance to the woods. Robbie Hedgehog had put his head between two bars and was peering down the path.

"I can't see him anymore," he reported to the others.

"He sure is brave," spoke up Wally. "I'd never be able to go in there on Hallowe'en night."

There were murmurs of agreement and, as the others resumed their vigil, Sarah and Roberta slipped silently away.

Roscoe had dropped his light swagger once he knew his friends could no longer see him. Even the older boys, Homer and Thad, had come to watch. He walked on, following the path, glancing around and now and then smiling to himself. Sarah and Roberta wouldn't be able to take him totally unawares -- they would make some noise, or probably giggle.

And he, Roscoe, would be prepared.

He glanced down at the mask in his hand. It was truly horrible -- great ugly warts, one eye bloodshot and glaring, the other sealed closed with a scar -- and the fangs, the beautiful fangs! He had fallen in love with the costume the moment he had seen it in Mr. Possum's store. It had taken nearly all the money in the bank he kept under his bed, but it was worth it, he thought, especially now.

Of course, he had not been able to wear the mask -- he didn't want to take a chance on Sarah or Roberta seeing it before they came wafting toward him. Then the tables would be turned! He would act as if he were running away, but would duck into the bushes and put on his mask, awaiting the perfect moment -- when they would be congratulating themselves! -- to leap out upon them.

Perfect! Twice in one Hallowe'en, and he could not possibly get in trouble!

Roscoe paused, peering through tree branches obscuring the path ahead. Was that something white drifting around the curve?

At the sudden crackling of twigs behind him, Roscoe whirled around.

Still in her ballerina costume, Sarah slipped up beside him.

"What are you doing here?" whispered Roscoe fiercely.

Sarah whispered back, "I just didn't want you to be alone, Roscoe."

Roscoe pursed his lips to keep a smile from his face. So it would be Roberta, then, approaching him and waving the curtains around. She'd probably start wailing and moaning, he thought dryly, and give herself away with her voice.

"Well, come on, then. I thought I saw something up ahead."

Sarah clutched Roscoe's paw tightly as they proceeded. She gave a little gasp and pointed down the path.

The moonlight silvered a vague white drifting shape in the distance.

"By the way," whispered Roscoe in amusement, "where's Roberta?"

"Right here," whispered Roberta back, appearing suddenly and silently at Roscoe's other side.

Roscoe froze and felt the hackles of his neck rising. His heart thumped loudly and there was a ringing in his ears.

Sarah and Roberta are here -- here with me -- he thought numbly.

And the ghost, he thought, gazing with wide and horrified eyes at the path in front of them, is there!

By now the dim and wavering figure had approached near enough that they could clearly detect its movement. A low moaning rose in volume until every hair on Roscoe's body felt as if it were standing on end.

"It's the ghost!" quavered Sarah. "It's all true!"

Roscoe stumbled backwards.

"Run!" he cried in a hoarse whisper. "Run!" He could get out no other words.

Grabbing his sisters, he rushed headlong, half leading, half dragging them, back the way they had come. He could hear the pounding of their feet -- or was that his own heartbeat?

But over it all, he could hear the terrifying moan which seemed closer than ever.

This was as fast as he could go -- Sarah and Roberta were slowing him down, and he could hear their frantic gasping as they alternately ran and stumbled.

Then Roberta's hand was wrenched from his grasp!

He turned in a spasm of fear; she had tripped and now lay in a little heap on the ground, too out of breath even to stand by herself.

Roscoe glanced up. The spirit was no more than 20 feet away, and its moaning seemed to be more high-pitched and -- and -- somehow -- vengeful. Knowing he was losing agonizing seconds, Roscoe threw a desperate look at Sarah, who had paused on the pathway ahead.

"Keep going!" he croaked, and turned back to help Roberta. He could not carry her. He would have to drag her.

Oh, how he regretted being here!

Gone were any thoughts of his mask, of his friends at the edge of the woods, that he was here 'proving his courage'!

All he wanted to do was get them safely out of there!

Roberta was hobbling along now, Roscoe frantically forcing her to hurry her pace. The wild moaning seemed to fill the woods around him.

Then he could hear voices -- relief swept over him -- the gate was in sight, and Sarah, beckoning him to hurry, to go faster. He put on a sudden, surprising burst of speed -- nothing could hurt them now, could it, in sight and presence of safety and his friends?

With a last gasp and leap, Roscoe was through the gateway!

He fell to his knees, bringing Roberta with him. The children clustered around them, trying to help him up.

"We heard it!"

"It was awful -- that moaning!"

"I don't know how you dared to go in there to begin with!"

Roscoe was still on the ground, his breathing and heartbeat slowly returning to normal. He looked up to see Sarah gazing at him solemnly. Roberta, beside him on the ground, was rubbing her ankle, a look of pain on her face. Roscoe tried to ask if she was all right, but his throat and mouth were dry and parched. He knew he could not stand yet -- his muscles still twitched from the terrifying flight through the woods.

After several minutes, the children gradually dispersed, heading slowly toward their homes and talking in hushed and shivery tones of Roscoe's great exploit and bravery.

Even Thad had remained until the end, looking a little shamefaced.

"I thought it was all a joke, Roscoe, but I actually heard

it! It gave me chills all over." Gazing at the woods, he muttered, "Maybe the little kids were right. Maybe there is something out there."

"I saw it, Thad."

Finally, even Thad was gone, and Roscoe rose to his feet, helping Roberta up as well. Then he caught sight of Sam hovering on the fringe of the departing schoolmates.

Roscoe narrowed his eyes. Sam hadn't been there when he had gone into the woods -- Roscoe had assumed he was still out Trick-or-Treating. And what was the bundle he was carrying under his arm?

Something soft -- something white -- something filmy.

Roscoe looked quickly at his sisters' faces. They fidgeted and would not meet his eyes. Roscoe flushed in sudden anger, and opened his mouth to say something wrathful. But his anger left him just as quickly as it had come.

After all, it was not their fault -- he had started it, hadn't he?

And when you thought about it, it was a pretty devious plot for his two younger sisters to figure out.

He almost smiled, but then his brow darkened as he thought of Sam. Well, Sam had only said he was not going to ever speak to him again. Nothing about moaning and wailing at him, or scaring him nearly to death!

"Well, we really got him back good," said Sarah, without much enthusiasm.

Roberta just nodded, testing weight on her injured ankle.

"What's wrong, Roberta?" asked Sarah anxiously. "Is it sprained?"

"No, no," responded Roberta. Then, more quietly, "You know, Sarah, Roscoe could have left me back on the path when I fell, but he didn't -- he wouldn't go on without me -"

"I know, I know!" whispered Sarah.

"I feel bad now."

"Me, too."

Both girls stood forlornly. Roscoe came up to them.

"Can you walk okay, Roberta?" he asked, reaching out to help.

"I'm okay, Roscoe. Sarah can help me."

Roberta, filled with guilt, stared at her toes.

"Are you okay?" she asked timidly, glancing up at him. She was surprised to see a smile on his face.

"What is it? What are you thinking?"

"Oh," said Roscoe vaguely, turning towards home. "I was just thinking of some good ideas for next Hallowe'en."

Roberta and Sarah exchanged highly indignant looks, then plodded tiredly behind him.

All they wanted at that moment was home and Mother and hot cocoa by the fire.

# VII - S'MORES AND MORE

"You get all that junk out of here, right now!" came Sarah's impassioned little voice from the bedroom.

"Oh, stop making such a fuss about it!" replied Roberta.

"How would you like it if you opened your bureau drawer and found..."

"What? A bunch of hair ribbons? Horrors!" interrupted Roberta.

"...a dirty old glove and ball? And your shoes are under my bed, and your dirty clothes are on my chair..."

Sam, at his desk in his own room, sniggered.

"If you want to live like that, why don't you go and

share a room with pigpen next door?" said Sarah angrily.

Sam straightened abruptly. Pigpen! Sarah was going too far! He looked around his room. It was still reasonably neat from Mother's housecleaning, but he decided it would be best to hide a few things he had added since then. He looked around again with a critical eye. He didn't think Mother would actually move Roberta in with him, but just in case, best to pick up his clothes and straighten the shelves a bit.

"I have had it," cried Sarah.

"Well, do something about it then," responded Roberta carelessly. Sam heard the squeak of springs as Roberta threw herself on her bed.

There was silence.

Sam returned to his book, only to be immediately interrupted by thumps against his wall.

"Mother!" yelled Roberta.

At the sound of his mother bustling up the staircase, Sam peered out of his own room.

"What is all this noise?" she demanded.

"Sarah made this line down the middle of the room, and threw all this stuff on my side..."

"Only her own stuff which was on my side," interjected a flushed and disheveled Sarah.

Mother Mouse looked at the girls in frustration.

"You know there isn't another bedroom. Can't you two manage to get along together?"

"I'm not the problem, Mother," said Roberta.

"Oh," said Sarah, turning on her sister, "and I suppose I am? It's not all my dirty junk all over the room and other peoples' beds."

"Stop calling my things JUNK!" yelled Roberta.

"Girls, girls!"

Sam cleared his throat.

"My room's very small, you know. I don't think anyone else could fit. And it's sort of neat, now..."

"Oh, be quiet, Sam," snapped Roberta.

Before he could reply, Mother said, "Go to your room, Sam," so brusquely that he quickly withdrew his head and slunk back to his desk. Picking up his book, he muttered under his breath.

"They better not try and move Roberta in here. I'll have a thing or two to say then." Sam continued to dwell on the dire consequences to all should he be made to share his room.

"Just look at what she's done, Mother," and Roberta swept her hand towards the center of the bedroom, down which, between the two beds, Sarah had taped a long piece of yarn.

"That's my half and that' said Sarah with curled lip, "is hers."

Except for the crumpled quilt, Sarah's side was neat, with shoes placed precisely by pairs in a row, her bureau drawers closed and her hair ribbons and purse and jewelry box neatly arranged on top. Even the pillow on her chair was plumped.

In contrast, Roberta's side looked as if a tornado had hit it. Noticing her mother's expression, Roberta said, "Sarah did it."

As Sarah began to bristle, Mother rushed to intervene.

"All right, all right, just stay calm."

"I am calm," said Roberta.

Sarah remained silent. Mother took a deep breath.

"Roberta, it is unpleasant enough when you have your own room and are not, well, not neat, but when you share a room you have to make some extra effort..."

"Tell her," said Roberta in a bored tone.

"Tell me!" squeaked Sarah.

Mother raised her voice.

"Silence!"

Both girls stopped abruptly. It was hard to remember when they had last seen a look of anger on their mother's face.

"I want this constant bickering to stop as of now. Roberta," and here Mother surveyed her side of the room, "you are to clean up your things before you go to bed tonight, and you, Sarah," she continued as her gaze swept to her other daughter, "you stop being such a - a - Miss Priss!"

At that, Mother swept from the room, leaving two subdued girls behind.

"Well," she thought ruefully, "I didn't handle that very well."

It didn't help Mother's mood very much when Sam followed her down the stairs.

"I really don't think Roberta's stuff would fit in my room," he said anxiously. "They have the biggest room now..."

"Go back to your bedroom, Sam!"

Sam returned to his room and fumed.

"They cause all the trouble, and I get sent to my room!"

Life was so unfair, he thought.

The subdued air lingered through the next morning. Speaking to each other as little as possible, Sarah and Roberta were excessively polite.

"Please pass the butter, Roberta -- that is, if you're not too tired from cleaning."

"Oh, certainly, Sarah. Just let me dust it first."

Needless to say, breakfast was a strained affair. Roscoe, who had been informed by Sam of what had transpired, muttered, "Better move over, you may have a roommate soon," and adding, as an after-thought, "Pigpen."

He received a kick on his ankle in reply, but with a

glance at his mother's face, decided not to make an issue of it.

Sarah lingered at breakfast so she would not have to walk with Roberta. She still smarted from her sister's remarks during breakfast, especially when, at an imaginary speck of dust on the tablecloth, Roberta had screamed, "Eek! Eek!" At her brothers' startled looks, she had pointed at the table. "Look! Dirt!"

The laughter had been at Sarah's expense, but she had snootily turned up her nose at the whole bunch of them.

Then, as Roberta was leaving, she had leaned over to Sarah and said in a loud theatrical whisper, "Be careful! You have to walk on the road to get to school, and I hear it's made of dirrrt! With all kinds of messy rocks and grass!" Roberta had swept from the room in a gust of laughter.

Trudging to school, Sarah continued to smolder about the previous evening's events. Mother's words had stung. Was she a "Miss Priss?" Just because she liked things neat and tidy, how did she end up somehow in the wrong?

And, she thought resentfully, most of Roberta's stuff -- at least what ended up on Sarah's side of the room -- was junk.

By the time she reached school, she had bolstered her sense of self-pity. She knew that she was right and Roberta was wrong, and that's all there was to it.

A group of the girls gathered outside the school in animated discussion. Sarah slowed down and was motioned over by Molly Beaver.

"Sarah, you'll never guess what!" exclaimed Molly with shining eyes.

"Patricia Possum's having a slumber party and we're all invited!" blurted Annie Rabbit, her nose twitching in excitement.

"Oooh!" breathed Sarah.

Patricia lived in a large, stately house with manicured gardens that bordered the wood. An only child, Patricia had her own bedroom. At the moment, that in itself was a matter of intense envy to Sarah.

But Patty's parents were wealthy and Patty was, perhaps, a little spoiled. Sarah sighed and yearned to be pampered and to have her own room, and all the pretty clothes that Patty had. Today she was wearing little pink slippers that matched her dress and hair bow. And Patty always seemed so confident and self-assured.

Patricia herself joined the group, no less enthusiastic than the others. The girls begged for details.

"Well," she said with a smile, "first we will have dinner -- roasted cashew nuts, boysenberries, creamed corn and other fruits and vegetables, all prepared by our cook."

They all knew of the Possum's famous cook. The children's mouths watered at the thought of eating foods they only had on special occasions, if then.

Patricia continued. "For dessert, s'mores, all gooey and dripping with chocolate and marshmallow. Then the games..."

Sarah's heart was nearly pounding out of her chest with the excitement of it all.

"Oh, Patricia!" she squealed in delight. "I can hardly wait! Roberta and I have never had s'mores before!"

There was a sudden silence.

"What's wrong?" asked Sarah, confused by her friends' abrupt change in demeanor.

Patricia responded in her usual confident way, placing her hand on Sarah's shoulder.

"Nothing, Sarah. It's -- it's just that the girls and I were talking..."

Sarah was alarmed. It was not like Patricia to be so hesitant.

Patricia took a deep breath and looked straight at Sarah.

"You see, Sarah, this is awkward, but we -- the girls and I -- decided that Roberta probably wouldn't enjoy the party, so we thought it best not to invite her."

Sarah was aghast.

"Not invite Roberta!" she cried.

"Shhh!" whispered Megan, and Betty Rabbit gestured to Sarah to keep her voice down. No one wanted Roberta to overhear.

"Why are you so surprised, Sarah?" continued Patricia gently. "You know that Roberta is a tomboy and likes things like baseball and climbing trees. Do you think she would really enjoy playing dolls and looking at clothes and all of that? We're not trying to be mean. We really don't think Roberta would have any fun at the party."

Sarah's eyes welled with tears.

"But Patty, just because Roberta likes these other things doesn't mean she wouldn't like to come to the party, too. Why, we do lots of things at home that...." Sarah's voice trailed off as she realized that she couldn't name even one thing that she and Roberta did together that would make her friends change their mind.

Roberta was a tomboy, she admitted to herself. Roberta successfully evaded any social event requiring that she wear a dress rather than her overalls. Troubled, Sarah turned away and entered the schoolroom.

* * * * *

Roberta, meanwhile, hardly noticed Sarah's somber mood and air of distraction during the day, for she was distracted as well.

"Mother was right," she grumbled to herself, "Sarah is a Miss Priss. All she thinks about is having everything neat. She doesn't even play with some of her things because they might get dirty."

"But she's always helping Mother -- while I'm outside playing," thought Roberta ruefully.

"And if it weren't for her, our room would be a mess. She's always putting my things away and dusting. Even making my bed when I forget.

In a sudden rush of affection and remorse, Roberta

planned something extra special for Sarah.

"A surprise," she thought. "Sarah is going to Molly Beaver's for dinner tonight, right from school. If I hurry home after school, I can get it all done before she comes home."

The rest of the day Roberta planned.

And when school was out, Roberta, full of ideas, rushed home.

That evening, tired but satisfied, Roberta looked around the bedroom at her handiwork. At the sound of the Beavers' pony cart, signaling Sarah's return, she jumped onto her bed and picked up a book, holding it in front of her face.

Listening acutely, she heard the murmur of voices downstairs, the clip-clop and rumble of the pony cart, and then Sarah's tread upon the stairs.

The door opened and there was a moment of silence.

Roberta peeked out from behind her book.

"Surprise!" she said.

She certainly did not expect the stricken look on Sarah's face.

"Oh, Roberta! It's -- it's beautiful!"

Roberta was puzzled. If it was so beautiful, what was with that look?

Sarah walked around the room, touching and admiring all the things Roberta had done.

The curtains, thought Sarah.

Instead of just hanging limply, they had been artfully looped back. With her hair ribbon, Sarah noticed.

Sarah looked at her dresser. How had Roberta managed to make it look so much nicer just by arranging things differently? Both the beds were neatly smoothed and pillows arranged invitingly. Roberta had left the yarn divider in place, but covered it with a soft chenille rug between the beds. Sarah recognized it as one from their mother's room.

I hope she asked first, thought Sarah, with her first smile since entering the room.

The lamps were on and flowers arranged in a vase on the desk, and everything was neat and clean, but, thought Sarah, much more. Looking around again, Sarah thought, why, Roberta has a flair for decorating.

Then she noticed the new object on her bureau and rushed over to it.

A large, gracefully branched twig had been sanded and painted, and set in a plaster base covered with tiny seashells. From the branches hung Sarah's assortment of ribbons and hair bows and bracelets, and her locket from Mother.

"Do you like it?" asked Roberta, holding her breath.

"Oh, Roberta," said Sarah, turning to her with tears in her eyes. "It's all so beautiful -- so special -- and the ribbon tree -- you made that? You used all your shell collection?"

Roberta, somewhat abashed at Sarah's emotion,

nodded, then raised one hand.

"I solemnly promise, Sarah," she said, "to keep all my junk neatly put away, to make my bed every day, and to really help keep our room clean."

"Roberta," cried Sarah, and reached out to her sister and hugged her.

*"Roberta," cried Sarah, and reached out to her sister and hugged her.*

"I'm so sorry for yelling at you and throwing your things around."

"I'm sorry, too, Sarah." Roberta smiled. "So we're friends again?"

"Best friends," smiled Sarah, wiping her eyes.

"Well, good thing," said Roberta impishly, "because if you had thrown me out, no one else would have taken me in!"

They both laughed, and Roberta showed Sarah other things she had done which were not so obvious, such as the bureau drawers with everything folded neatly, and one drawer reserved, said Roberta, opening it to show Sarah, for all her "junk."

They continued to giggle, and admire, and exclaim until Mother called up to ask why they weren't in bed.

"Good night, Sarah," said a happy Roberta, snuggling under her quilt.

Soon the only lights were the stars in the night sky and a big hazy moon rising on two little mice tucked in their beds, sound asleep.

* * * * *

In the morning, however, Sarah moped about the house. Mother Mouse watched with anxious eyes. Was Sarah getting sick?

By Sunday evening, Mother was ready to call Dr. Raccoon.

"Are you feeling warm, Sarah?" she asked, putting her hand on Sarah's forehead.

Sarah pulled away.

"I'm all right, Mother," she answered listlessly. "I'm just tired. I think I'll go to bed."

Mother watched as Sarah trudged up the stairs.

She was not at all surprised when the following morning Roberta bounded down the steps and announced, "Sarah says she has a cold and can't go to school."

Once the other children were gone, Mother mounted the stairs to Sarah's room, thermometer in hand.

"Oh, Mother," said Sarah pettishly, turning away. "I don't need that, honest."

"Well, something's wrong, Sarah. Don't you want to talk about it?"

"I just don't feel good," said Sarah in a tone that ended discussion.

Mother Mouse sighed and decided to leave Sarah to herself for a while.

Roberta walked to school, smiling to herself as she relived the previous evening's surprise and Sarah's reaction. Mounting the school steps, she was stopped by Molly Beaver.

"Where's Sarah, Roberta?"

"Oh, she's sick and not coming to school today," responded Roberta casually.

"Sick! Oh, I hope she's well by Saturday so she won't miss the party!"

Roberta turned toward Molly.

"Party? What party?"

Molly stood, stricken.

"Ah, just any party -- I don't know -- maybe there'll be a party sometime..."

Her voice trailed off as she and Roberta stared at each other.

The bell rang loudly and Molly broke away and hastened with relief up the steps, leaving Roberta in turmoil.

Somehow Roberta got through the day, a smile pasted on her face. Now the groups of chattering girls at recess took on new meaning, and she strained to pick up phrases here and there.

Apparently there was a party. It seemed as if every girl in class, including Sarah, knew about it and was invited.

Except Roberta.

Roberta managed to walk home and slam the door behind her before she dropped her smile. Mother found her there and stopped in concern at the pale, drawn face.

"Roberta, you're not sick, too, are you?"

To Mother's amazement, Roberta burst into tears and sobbed long and hard.

"Oh, Mother," she hiccuped. "They're having a party and didn't invite me. And Sarah's going, and how could she go without me? I hate them all!"

Roberta continued to sob while Mother Mouse tried ineffectually to console her.

Well, thought Mother, this explains Sarah's mysterious "cold."

At a slight sound from above, Mother looked up to see Sarah staring at them wide-eyed from the staircase.

"Roberta knows about the party, Sarah," said Mother softly.

Sarah flew to her mother.

"I'm not going, Mommy. I wasn't going to the party. They're so mean! How could they not invite Roberta? Patty even invited that old Joelle Muskrat..."

"Sarah!" warned Mother.

"I'm sorry, but I just don't like her, Mother. She's not going anyway. But except for her, Roberta would have been about the only girl in the whole school who wasn't going!"

At this, Roberta wailed louder.

Mother sat comforting the two sobbing girls until she was forced to extricate herself to answer the very loud knocking at the door.

Robbie Hedgehog stood on the steps, holding out a large envelope.

"Mrs. Possum gave me ten cents if I would run right down and give this to you," he said matter-of-factly.

"Why, thank you, Robbie," said Mother, taking the envelope from his hand.

Robbie dashed off and Mother closed the door. She turned the envelope in her hand.

She opened it slowly, then smiled as she read its contents.

Well, thought Mother, what a very gracious and tactful thing to do.

"Roberta," said Mother to the two little girls clutching each other in the big chair. "There's a note here for you."

Roberta looked at her with swollen eyes.

"I don't care about any old note," she said, rather unconvincingly, interested in spite of herself. To get something delivered just to her was rather a novelty.

Come to think of it, she realized, it was a first.

"I think you'll be interested once you see it," smiled Mother.

Roberta took the small envelope and carefully opened it, Sarah looking on with curiosity.

"Mommy, would you read it to me? It's in handwriting," she said anxiously, handing the note to her mother.

Mother Mouse held the note out elegantly, reading it slowly and enunciating every syllable, as if she were announcing a ball at the King's court.

"To Miss Roberta Mouse. Patricia has brought it to my attention that I inadvertently neglected to send you an invitation to the sleep-over party next Saturday. Please accept the enclosed, along with my sincere apologies. I look forward to seeing you and Sarah at the party."

"Why, it's an invitation!" said Roberta, looking from Mother to Sarah, eyes shining through her tears. "It's an invitation to Patricia's party!"

"Somehow," said Mother, looking at Sarah with a little nod, "your invitation had been overlooked."

Sarah and Roberta turned to each other delightedly.

"Now we can both go," they exclaimed together, then laughed with the excitement of the whole thing.

* * * * *

The day of the party finally came.

Sarah had been planning every detail for days, of course, and was in such a state of euphoria that she was beside herself. Her bedroll was neatly tied and her comb and toothbrush tucked into her cosmetic bag. Her mother had given it to her a year ago, but she had never had a reason to use it until now, her first special occasion outside of home. Her best dress was laundered, pressed, and smelled sweetly of the lavender sachet that Mother had hung in her closet.

Roberta planned to wear her best trousers, as she had never seen the need to even have a dress. Sarah sighed in resignation, not having the heart to tell her sister that she would be conspicuous. She suspected that Roberta would not have cared, anyway.

Sarah was waiting downstairs for Roberta, sitting carefully in Mother's big chair so as not to rumple her party dress. Occasionally she looked down at her shiny slippers and frilled socks, or patted the bow on her head to make sure it was still in place.

"Oh, don't you look lovely!" said Mother as she came down the stairs and entered the room.

Sarah beamed with the praise and, if possible, looked even lovelier.

"Roberta," called Mother, "please come down -- you'll be late for the party!"

With the sound of rustling petticoats, Roberta appeared on the landing in a beautiful new dress.

She was gorgeous! Sarah hardly recognized her.

"Is that you, Roberta?" she asked in disbelief.

Roberta giggled. Her mother, who was of course in on the surprise, beamed on the two girls.

It was not only Sarah that was surprised.

Roberta was the rage of the party!

The next morning, after a late breakfast, the girls chattered excitedly as they packed up their belongings to return home.

"It was so much fun, Patty!" said Annie Rabbit, echoed by her sisters Betty and Cassie.

"Well, a lot of the fun was due to Roberta's ideas," said Patty sincerely.

"Yes," said Molly with enthusiasm, "It's fun to play with paper dolls -- especially your new ones, Patty -- but when Roberta thought of having a store where we buy our clothes..."

"With Monopoly money," laughed Betty.

"That just made it more fun."

Megan Squirrel piped up, "I liked the idea about the doll hospital."

Turning to Roberta, she asked, "Can you really fix our broken dolls?"

"Sure," answered Roberta confidently, "and what I can't fix, Roscoe can."

"Oooh!" said Megan and Cassie together, for they had discussed the boys the previous evening in their whispered conversations. Although they agreed that Robbie Hedgehog's new haircut made him look "like a movie star" and that Wally Mole's new glasses made him look "intellectual," it was Roscoe that all the girls (to Roberta's secret disgust and Sarah's silent amusement) thought was who they'd most like to go on a date with -- when they were old enough, of course. A great part of his appeal was, apparently, that he was one of the "big boys."

"Well," sighed Betty, "it was all fun -- the charades, the fashion show. It was so great of your mother to let us dress up in all those glamorous clothes, Patty!"

Amidst all the good-byes and farewells (as if they were not going to see one another again the next morning), Mrs. Possum came out to see the girls off, thanking each one for coming.

Turning to Roberta, she said in a very heartfelt manner (for after all, Mrs. Possum had been a little apprehensive, not quite sure what to expect after hearing tales of Roberta's outlandish adventures), "Thank you so much for helping to make Patricia's party a success. I hope you'll come to visit again soon."

Sarah and Roberta were delighted and giggled all the way home.

Roberta immediately ran upstairs to change into her overalls, while Sarah lingered to provide her Mother's willing ears with all the details, replete with descriptions of the Possums' furnishings, the food, the gleaming chandeliers, how each of the girls were dressed, and again, several times, the food.

Roberta came down the stairs looking her usual self, but stopped when Sarah called out to her.

"Where are you going, Roberta?"

"Outside," said Roberta, "and I'm going to just run, and run, and maybe climb a tree, and won't have to worry about getting anything on my clothes," she added fervently.

Sarah grinned, then took her aside out of Mother's hearing.

"Did you notice that arrangement of dried flowers and seed pods on Mrs. Possum's buffet? It was probably very expensive, but, you know, I think we could make one just as good for Mother. That is," she added, "if you could help me find them."

Roberta thought a moment, then grinned widely.

"I know a bunch of places to find them, Sarah. We'll have to wait for Spring for the wildflowers -- there'll be plenty out by the big rock in the meadow, and you know where that old statue of the deer is in the woods? Well -"

"Show me," said Sarah. "Just let me change clothes."

Darting up the stairs, she stopped and turned.

"Can I wear a pair of your overalls?"

Roberta crinkled her eyes and nodded. "And bring our mittens and jackets!"

They were silent as they trudged through the fields towards the woods.

"Do you remember…" began Sarah hesitantly.

"Remember what?" asked Roberta.

"When Daddy used to call me his Little House Mouse, and he called you his Little Field Mouse?"

"Yes," said Roberta quietly, "I remember."

"You know, he didn't love either one of us more, he loved us all the same, even Sam and Roscoe when he knew it was Sam who loved books and studying like he did."

After a moment, Roberta said, "I remember Daddy saying one time he wished he had only half of Roscoe's energy and enthusiasm."

"So he loved us all, in spite of our differences," responded Sarah.

"And maybe because of them," added Roberta after a moment's silence.

Sarah took Roberta's paw and gave it a squeeze.

"I'm glad we're sisters," she said.

"And twins," said Roberta in mock surprise.

Laughing and calling back and forth, they chased each other through the tall grasses of the meadow on their way to the woods.

# VIII - Christmas Presents (And Pasts)

"Mother, when can we get the Christmas boxes down from the attic?" asked Roberta.

It was Saturday and only two weeks before Christmas, so Mother's only surprise was that Roberta had been able to wait this long.

"I think it may be time right now, Roberta," said Mother with a twinkle in her eye. "Bring the wooden ladder from the shed so we can reach them. This afternoon we can get the tree and tonight we can all decorate it.

"Yippee!" squealed Roberta in ecstasy.

She ran to the shed and hauled the ladder into the house. As she ascended to the attic, Mother listened uneasily for the sounds of wood against wood or, more alarmingly, the tinkle of fragile items. She sighed with relief when she heard Roberta say, "There!"

Sarah rushed from the kitchen when she heard the noise.

"We're getting the Christmas decorations out?" she asked, spying the ladder.

Roberta nodded in excitement.

"Oh, Roberta, I'll make fudge with lots of walnuts for tonight's tree trimming," said Sarah excitedly.

"And we'll have hot chocolate with marshmallows -"

"And tea with cream -"

"And those little cakes with the jelly and glaze -"

"Whoa!" said Mother. "We'll have to go out to get the tree this afternoon."

"Oh, Mother, I'll start right now."

And Sarah flew into the kitchen, but then popped her head out.

"Don't open anything until I come back," she said anxiously.

"Don't worry," smiled Mother, "I'll help you with the baking as soon as the boxes are down, then we'll open them together."

Soon Mother was seated in her big chair and the two girls were on the living room floor, carefully unsealing boxes and pulling out items.

"Look, Mother, here's the Santa doll I made for you when I was little," exclaimed Roberta. "It's so funny looking!"

"And this," said Sarah, holding up an object and regarding it curiously. "It looks like food."

Mother smiled. "Sam made that his first year in school." She peered at it more closely. "I think it's macaroni glued onto cardboard, then glitter sprinkled on it."

At the girls' giggles, Mother said a bit defensively, "It was very beautiful when he brought it home, and he was so proud of it."

"Okay," laughed Roberta, "I won't make fun of Sam's decoration -- look at this!"

She held up the tree ornament she had made by winding yarn around a toilet tissue roll. "It still looks like a toilet paper roll!"

The many fragile ornaments collected over the years were placed on the table. The homemade ones were examined seriously by Sarah and Roberta.

"I really think this one should go on the back of the tree," said Roberta severely.

Sarah snatched it from her.

"Oh, Mother, this is the one I made from a dried apple --

see, it looks like a little old lady! She just wants it on the back of the tree because it's one I made!"

Roberta lifted out a piece of felt which had once had bright-colored letters glued to it spelling out Merry Christmas.

"Well, here's one I made, and I don't care if it goes on the tree at all. Who wants something that says 'er y t as' hanging on your tree?" she retorted.

"Oh, okay," responded Sarah, peering more closely at the dried apple face. "I think she's lost her eyes, anyway."

Mother picked up the rejected tree decorations and placed them in a small pile on her end table.

"For our keepsake box," she said with a smile at the girls' questioning glances.

Finally all that remained was one small sturdily built box. It was carefully unsealed.

"Here's the cottage that Daddy made," said Sarah wistfully, "the one that looks like our house all decorated for Christmas."

She looked at all the detail. "The door still opens," she added quietly, handing it to her mother who placed it in the center of the mantel.

"We'll take very good care of it so that you can share it with your own little ones some day," said Mother gently.

That afternoon the Mouse family, bundled up in hats,

mittens, scarves, and jackets, left the house and started out on the road to the woods. Sam pulled Skitch in the sled, and Roscoe carefully carried the hatchet for cutting down the tree.

It was clear and sunny but with a nip in the air, and Mother hoped that it wouldn't take too long to find the "perfect" tree.

"How about that one over there?" asked Sarah, pointing to one on the horizon, about as far, Mother judged, as the human eye could possibly discern an object.

"Too tall," said Roscoe, after they got closer, "but that one over there is just right!"

"No," said Roberta, after they had walked about a quarter of a mile in another direction, "it's too short and has a bare spot."

They continued on from one tree to another in a zig-zag course that left Mother totally disoriented. Weren't they back near the gate again? Hadn't she seen that tree already? It looked awfully familiar.

Oh, well, they'll get less picky as the afternoon wears on, Mother consoled herself.

Mother sighed in relief when finally the perfect tree was discovered. It was about the right height, they figured, was full and lush with no empty spots, and perfectly shaped all around.

Then they stood back while Roscoe brought the tree down and loaded it onto the sled from which Skitch, unwillingly, had been removed. Sam started pulling the sled and tree toward home, while Skitch was positioned for a piggy -back ride on Roscoe.

With Sam leading, Mother and Roscoe bringing up the rear and the twins arm in arm between them, they shortened the walk home by singing Christmas carols. Even Skitch joined in, making up in volume what he lacked in intelligibility.

"Mother, look what the Beavers left on the doorstep!" called Sam as he approached the door.

"These are the most beautiful I've seen yet!" exclaimed Mother at the sight of the large mound of greenery and berries for decorating. "They have really outdone themselves this year."

She and the girls carried armfuls of the fir and pine and holly inside.

"Are the berries really poison, Mother?" asked Sam.

"Heavens, no! Mrs. Beaver wouldn't send over anything like that with Skitch in the house!"

Sam gave Roberta an odd look and she glanced at Mother shamefaced.

"I just wanted him to leave them alone, at least until they've been up for a few days."

"All right," laughed Mother. "We'll have to make a new rule for the Christmas season: no eating the decorations."

As dusk approached, Mother and Sarah started dinner while Roscoe, Sam, and Roberta wrestled the tree into the living room next to the fireplace.

"I think the tree grew since we cut it," said Sam uncertainly.

"It does seem taller," said Roscoe. "But that's okay, I can fix it," he added cheerfully. "I'll just cut some off of it."

Roscoe sawed away and once more they stood the tree upright.

"Roscoe, do you think maybe you should have cut it off the other end?" asked Roberta slowly. "It looks sort of -- well, sort of squat."

Roscoe looked at the tree critically.

"I think you're right," he said glumly, looking from the tree to the treetop on the floor.

Then he brightened.

"But you know what? Now we can make a little tree and put it upstairs!"

"In whose room?" asked Roberta coldly.

"Well, I'm the one who thought of cutting the tree."

"Ruining the tree, you mean."

"Look, Roberta, if you think you're such a..."

"Children!"

The three of them whirled around.

Mother stood before them.

"I can't believe you are all here wrangling about the

Christmas tree. This is something that should be done in joy and love -"

"Look at the tree, Mother," said Roberta.

Mother looked.

"It -- what happened?"

*"I think the tree grew since we cut it," said Sam uncertainly.*

Roberta gave her brother an I-told-you-so look.

"I think it's going to be a beautiful tree, Roscoe," said Mother reassuringly. "Just wait until all the ornaments and lights and tinsel are on it and you'll see."

"I know," smiled Roberta, mollified. "It's like magic."

She smiled at Roscoe, who grinned back.

"Well, I can start stringing the popcorn and cranberries," offered Sam.

"No!" said Roscoe and Roberta in unison.

"You always eat so many of them that the garlands look skimpy," Roberta said in an annoyed tone. "We'll all do them together."

Sam, disgruntled, returned to perusing the books which Mother brought out only at Christmas time, the special copies of "A Night Before Christmas," "The Magi," and "A Christmas Carol."

Mother and Sarah soon produced pewter trays piled with goodies. By then everyone was so hungry that the tree was forgotten for a while. It was somehow special to get to snack on so many things without having to worry about whether they ate their vegetables or had to suffer through helpings of something they didn't like. Everything tasted good.

And then they gathered by the fire for their traditional tree-trimming ritual.

Mother carefully arranged the lights and then Roscoe and Sam, in turn, handed Roberta and Sarah the ornaments. Placing them on the tree, the girls would recite past Christmas remembrances associated with each one.

There was much laughter when they came to the decorations they had each made in previous years and friendly compromises about what would go on the tree and where.

"Oh, Mother, Skitch is ruining everything!" wailed Roberta.

Scooping him up from the tangle of tinsel and tissue paper in which he sat happily immersed, Mother took Skitch on her lap. She removed the tinsel dangling from his ears and the tip of his nose and popped a big piece of fudge in his mouth.

"There, that will keep him busy for a while," she said.

The tree was finally completed, the fir and pine boughs placed over the mantle and formed into a wreath for the door, and the sprigs of mistletoe that Roscoe had collected in the woods hung in strategic spots. Then, while they had second helpings of all the little cakes and rolls and tarts, and more hot chocolate, Mother turned on the Christmas tree lights.

Everything took on a mystical enchantment. Even the worn, homemade decorations on the tree, mellow in the golden glow, contributed to the homey, comfortable feeling. The evergreen scents from the tree and the green boughs draped about the room were distinctly those of Christmas.

They all sat and gazed at the tree, mesmerized by the transformation of their small cottage into a wonderland. It seemed that if you looked at it long enough, you would be transported to some magical kingdom where all wishes came true.

"Remember when Daddy -" began Sarah.

Then she stopped. Of course they remembered everything about Daddy.

Mother stroked her head lovingly and in silence for a few seconds as each of them held their own special thoughts of their father at this time of year.

"Oh, my goodness," said Mother, "Skitch has fallen fast asleep. And -"

"Oh, Mother," they groaned, "just a little while longer!"

"All right," she smiled. "I'll take Skitch up to bed and get things cleaned up in the kitchen, but then, I want you all upstairs."

The short reprieve satisfied them and they sat again before the tree, finishing off the last of the treats, and dreaming of Christmases past and planning for Christmas present.

* * * * * *

The children had been preparing for some time to make a special gift for Mother.

Roberta had been to the village chandler's and taken notes. Sarah and Sam saved their allowance to buy paraffin. Roscoe, having spent all his money on his

Hallowe'en mask, was responsible for obtaining string from the butcher and a big cardboard ice cream container from the creamery. Sam collected bay leaves from the old tree by the river.

The Saturday before Christmas, while Mother was out, they had put together their creation. Sarah would not let Roberta into the kitchen at all, deeming it too dangerous to have her around the stove while the wax was being melted. But when the boys carried the big pot out to the back porch, Roberta was the one who directed the pouring and held the wick in place and generally ordered everyone around. After all, it had been her idea and she was the expert!

When it had hardened and cooled and the container had been removed, they all sat back and admired the huge candle.

"Mother will be so surprised and pleased," said Roberta, hardly able to contain her excitement.

"This is the best gift we have ever given her," crowed Sarah.

Roscoe had smoothed out the brown wrapping paper and Sarah had made a huge bow of cream-colored ribbon. It was carefully wrapped and hidden under Sam's bed.

"No one would ever find it in all this stuff," commented Sarah with satisfaction.

Sam gave her a disgusted look, but Roscoe and Roberta agreed it was the perfect hiding place, so there it stayed.

At dinner that night, Mother was unusually silent. It put a bit of a damper on the children's Christmas spirit.

Finally Sarah asked, "Mother, what's wrong?"

Mother looked up quickly.

"Nothing, Sarah, nothing. It's just, well, I had an idea to make our Christmas more meaningful, and I was just thinking of how to present it to you all."

They exchanged excited looks, and sat up in anticipation. How to make Christmas more special!

"You all know the Muskrat family who lives down by the river, don't you?"

Roscoe frowned.

"Well, I know Joelle. She's the same age as me."

"Nick and Ned started school the same time Roberta and I did," said Sarah slowly, not sure she liked where this was all leading.

"They're stuck up," said Roberta.

"What do you mean, Roberta?" asked Mother in consternation.

"Oh, they won't eat lunch with anyone -- they just go off together and share their lunch and never make trades with anyone else."

"And they don't talk much to anyone, either," added Sam.

"They don't wear shoes even in the cold weather, and they have all these mismatched patches on their clothes," said fastidious little Sarah.

Mother paused for a moment while the children waited expectantly.

"Mr. Muskrat is a carpenter, but he had an injury a few months ago and can't work, other than a few odd repair jobs he gets now and then. Joelle takes care of her brothers and little Talia, mends their clothes, and does most of the cooking and cleaning. It is hard for her to keep up with all of this and schoolwork as well."

"Why doesn't her mother just do all of that stuff?" asked Roberta impatiently.

"Mrs. Muskrat passed away of pneumonia about a year ago, and now it is just Father Muskrat, Joelle, the twins and Talia, who's only a toddler."

Roberta was abashed.

"I'm sorry," she said in a low voice, "I didn't know."

All of the children were silent, a bond of sympathy already growing between the fatherless Mouse family and the Muskrat children who had lost their mother.

"I remember," said Sarah, wrinkling her brow in thought, "when you had Roberta and me help carry over the basket of vegetables to their house. They were talking about the pies Mrs. Beaver had given them and the preserves Mrs. Squirrel had dropped off."

Her voice dropped.

"I thought they were beggars."

"Oh, Sarah," laughed Mother a little sadly, "I should have explained to you. All I knew was that you were very uncomfortable, so I never asked you to go with me again."

There was an awkward silence again.

"Well," continued Mother, "my idea -- if you all agree, that is -- is to invite the Muskrat family for Christmas dinner."

There were several exclamations, but no one responded. The Muskrats for Christmas dinner? They all felt uneasy at having a lot of people they hardly knew coming over for one of their most special family holidays.

Then Roscoe spoke up clearly.

"I think it's a great idea, Mother. I'm only sorry I didn't know the situation before, because I'm sure I could have helped out some over there. It must be hard for the little boys to do all the outside chores."

Mother gave Roscoe a loving look, full of relief and pride.

The others took their lead from Roscoe.

"All right, Mother, we'll make it a very special dinner, and we'll be on our best behavior and everything." said Roberta, receiving a grateful smile from Mother in return.

"I wish there was some way we could give them presents," said Sarah, "things they need, I mean. Then it wouldn't be so much like -"

"Begging?" interrupted Sam.

Sarah's face flamed.

"Not begging," said Mother softly. "Charity. And a love and concern for the wellbeing of one's neighbors. Neither the giver nor the recipient need be ashamed of that."

"Mother," intervened Roberta, "I just got my new winter shoes, but my old ones are still in good shape, you know it was just that I had outgrown them. I know Joelle is older than me, but she's so little -"

"Yes," nodded Mother, "I think they would fit her. And all polished up, they'll almost look new." Her eyes twinkled. "In fact, they are almost new. There are others besides Joelle who don't always wear their shoes in cold weather."

Roberta laughed, and that started them all thinking furiously of things they might be able to provide the Muskrat children.

"I have a lot of toys I've outgrown, but they'd be just right for Nick and Ned," said Sam.

He paused.

"I just have to find them," he added.

Everyone groaned.

"Don't worry, don't worry," he hastened to say. "I can find them. Some of them," he added huffily, looking at Sarah, "might even be under my bed."

"Well," said Mother, "I knitted Skitch two sweaters for this winter, but I'm sure he can get by without one of them. He and Talia are about the same size. And I have all the canned vegetables and dried fruits -- they can take some of them home with them."

"I don't have anything to give them," said Roscoe, "but I can chop firewood and do some of the heavy work around their house, and repair the front fence."

Mother beamed at him.

"Perfect, Roscoe! Oh, this couldn't have gone any better. I'm so happy!"

The children, faces wreathed in smiles, looked at each other. What fun they were going to have, making all their plans!

It was quickly agreed that Sam would make up a poem for the invitation, that Roscoe would deliver it and at the same time make his offer of assistance around the house. Sarah would help with the extra baking and cooking during the week that would be necessary for the additional guests at Christmas dinner, and Roberta would run the errands for the needed supplies.

Sam had already drawn a stool up to the hearth, and sat with tablet and pencil, gazing into the fire and waiting for inspiration.

Roberta wrote her list as Mother ticked them off.

"You'll need to go into the woods for more nuts and berries -- but don't go too far away from the path, Roberta.

Then, go to Mrs. Squirrel's and ask for a couple of jars of her nut butter and nut jelly. Then, let me see -"

"You wanted me to get some packets of seasoning herbs from Mrs. Hedgehog," added Roberta helpfully.

"Right. Put that down. Then, I'll need a couple of more baking tins from Mr. Possum's store -"

"I can ask Annie or Betty to tell their father so he can bring them home from the store and I can pick them up at the Rabbits' house."

"Fine," said Mother. She thought for a moment. "I might even ask Mrs. Mole if she would bake one of her double chocolate cakes. I'll run over tomorrow and ask her what ingredients she'll need."

Mother looked around at the children.

"Well, we're all ready to start tomorrow," she smiled.

Sam came up to her and handed her a sheet torn from his tablet.

"I just wanted to see if this is okay. I'm going to copy it out neatly and then Roscoe can deliver it."

"Oh, Sam, I'm so proud of you -- I'm proud of all of you."

"If you get it written up, Sam, I can deliver it tomorrow," said Roscoe. I may be a little late -- is that okay? If I start on some things over there?"

"That will be fine, Roscoe, but don't try to do too much," she responded a bit anxiously. She knew her son's deep kindness and well-meaning enthusiasm could lead him to take on more than he could comfortably handle.

"Don't worry, Mother!" he laughed.

"And I'll start my errands tomorrow," said Roberta.

"And I'll get all our recipes together for the baking," said Sarah.

"All right, all right," laughed Mother. "It looks like tomorrow is going to be a very busy day. So now -- bedtime!"

* * * * *

The next few days found the Mouse family rushing about in a whirlwind.

The Muskrats had accepted the invitation with surprised gratitude, and Roscoe was now spending a good portion of each day at their home, performing the chores that were his contribution. Sam had spent half of one day in his room, from which emerged a lot of thumping and bumping and muttered exclamations. He finally descended the stairs triumphantly carrying an armload of toys, which he unceremoniously dumped on the living room floor.

"Well, Sam," asked Mother, "what are you going to do with them now?"

"Me?"

Sam looked at the pile, then at his mother.

He sighed.

"Okay, okay, I'll clean them up and mend the ones that need it," he said reluctantly.

"If you don't want to give them up, Sam -"

"No, no. It's just that I didn't realize it was going to be so much work to give away things."

Mother and Sarah spent most of their days in the kitchen or at the dining room table in consultation over recipes, while Roberta had the time of her life running back and forth between home, the village store, the woods, and neighbors' houses.

One afternoon, looking for Sarah to review her "to-do" list, Roberta found her sister in their bedroom.

"Sarah, I -" burst out Roberta, then stopped as she saw Sarah quickly hide a small package in her bureau drawer.

Secrets were all part of the Christmas magic, so Roberta pretended she hadn't seen, and went on to discuss her list with Sarah.

But Sarah seemed withdrawn and showed no enthusiasm even when discussing the type and size of baking tins needed.

"What's wrong, Sarah?" asked Roberta.

"Oh, nothing," responded Sarah reluctantly. "Well, it was just something I was thinking of, but I'm not sure I really want to do it, and -- well, it doesn't just affect me..."

"Oh, for crying out loud, Sarah, just say it, I've got a million things to do!"

Sarah turned to the bureau and took out the small package she had placed in the drawer. It was a gift, wrapped in white paper and red ribbon, and Sarah turned it over and over in her hand as she spoke.

"It's a gift for you, Roberta, something I made. I was just thinking, I have plenty of time to make another one for you-"

"And you want to give this to Joelle!"

Sarah looked up quickly.

"Oh, not if it would hurt your feelings, Roberta, that's why I said it wasn't just me that I was thinking of -"

"I think it's a great idea, Sarah," exclaimed Roberta, her face alight with excitement. "And you know what? We've all got gifts for each other, and if we get Roscoe and Sam in on this, you know, we could come up with more gifts for the boys and Talia, too!"

"But how do you think they'll feel about this?"

"Let's ask them! Look, we all get each other things. If each one of us takes a gift we were going to give the other and gives it to one of the Muskrats instead, it'll just mean one less present for us, that's all."

"Let's find the boys," cried Sarah, starting for the door.

"Wait a minute," said Roberta, and Sarah turned around.

"What?" said Sarah.

"Well," said Roberta diffidently, "what was my gift?"

"Oh, Roberta," laughed Sarah, "do you want me to unwrap it and show you?"

"No, that's okay, I just wanted to know what I'm giving up!"

"All right, it's an embroidered bag to keep your comb and barrettes or hairpins."

"Oh," sighed Roberta in relief, "girl's stuff."

Sarah looked at her indignantly.

"Maybe I won't make you another one after all!"

"Oh, come on, Sarah," coaxed Roberta, "I was just teasing! Let's go get Roscoe and Sam!"

Once they had explained the plan, the boys agreed in characteristic fashion: Roscoe thought it was a great idea and immediately approved; Sam thought and fidgeted and had to make a list of how many gifts each one would get with and without donating one to the Muskrat family.

The others had sat making impatient sounds while he pondered the matter, but when he finally agreed, Roberta snorted, "Okay, so we'll each get two gifts instead of three, and Skitch will get three instead of four. I could have told you that 10 minutes ago!"

Then they sat down to figure out the details, writing out the gifts they had for each other, shielding their lists so no one could see, and speaking in cryptic sentences.

"Now," said Roscoe, "Sarah's giving her gift for Roberta to Joelle, so now the boys and Talia need something, but not from Sarah."

"I have a thing for Roscoe which I could give Nick or Ned," said Sam cautiously, "but we don't want it to be better than the gift whoever else gives to the twins."

"Why do you just assume your gift for Roscoe is better than anything else one of us got for you or Roscoe?" demanded Roberta.

"I didn't mean that," said Sam with exasperation, "I just want the gifts to be equal."

"My gift for Skitch really wouldn't be good for a girl -" began Roscoe.

"What is it?" asked Roberta.

" A baseball."

" A baseball? For Skitch? He's only a baby! What do you expect him to do with a baseball?"

"Well, he can -"

"He can throw it around and conk us on our heads!" said Roberta in disgust. "Now," she said, turning to Sarah, "I have this darling little pig that winds up -"

Roscoe looked at Sam.

"What was my gift?"

"Marbles."

Roscoe roared with laughter, startling the others into silence.

"I was giving you marbles!" he said.

Sam smiled. "Okay, good. We can give the gifts we would have given each other to Nick and Ned, Talia will get Skitch's pig from Roberta, and Joelle will get a gift from Sarah."

"Agreed?" asked Roscoe, looking at the others.

"Agreed," they all smiled.

# IX - CHRISTMAS MAGIC

On Christmas Eve the Mouse family gathered together in their cozy cottage. Darkness came early on winter evenings, and they were sitting around the fireplace enjoying the familiar Christmas customs and rituals and munching on the special snacks Mother always made for this most special of all nights.

They sang carols and told Skitch all about Santa, then sat in thoughtful silence while Mother told them again the story of Christmas: the little family turned away from the inn, finding shelter only in a stable; the glorious joy when the little baby was born and the choir of angels appeared to the shepherds in the field; and the great wonder of the three wise men kneeling before the holy child.

Sarah had realized that this year was the first Christmas without Father, which filled her with sadness. But after the Christmas story was told, she looked around at her brothers and sister and mother, and felt a quiet joy steal into her. She felt wrapped in the warmth of her family. She knew that Father would never be truly absent from their gatherings as long as they remembered him with love.

* * * * *

The sun had not yet risen and there was only the faintest haze of light on the horizon when Roscoe slipped downstairs to quietly bring in wood and get a fire going in the fireplace. To his surprise, the Christmas tree lights were on. He peeked into the kitchen and found Sarah, still in her nightgown and slippers, placing a pan in the oven. The big kettle was already steaming and she had laid out the honey, butter, marmalade, and cream on a tray, ready to be taken into the dining room.

Roscoe laid a finger across his lips and Sarah smiled in conspiratorial silence.

It was not long before they heard scuffling and whispers on the stairs and Roberta and Sam descended to find the dining room table set, a fire blazing on the hearth.

"I brought down Mother's present," whispered Sam, and Roberta took it from him and placed it under the tree.

"Oh, look!" she said. "There are presents here! This one's for you, Sam -- and here's another one."

Sarah and Sam had rushed over and were now down on their knees also, breathlessly examining the gifts and looking at labels.

"Quick, it's Mother and Skitch!" warned Roscoe, and the three of them heaped the gifts back into place under the tree and rushed to the staircase.

"Merry Christmas, Mother!" they chorused as she appeared on the landing, holding Skitch's paw and helping him descend the stairs.

Mother looked up with a big smile.

"Merry Christmas!"

She cocked her head.

"What's that I smell? And how nice and warm it is!"

"We've got the fire going, Mother, and breakfast is ready, so hurry!"

Mother had to be settled in the big armchair with a cup of tea, and with Skitch in her lap to prevent him from wreaking havoc on the glistening and beribboned packages. The children were too excited to eat and only waited until Mother was comfortable before turning their attention to the presents.

Soon tissue paper and bows and ribbons were piled in mounds around them. Roberta had decorated her gifts with small pine cones and bits of greenery, so Skitch was given them to keep him busy.

"Oh, Mother!" exclaimed Sarah, "I love it!

She drew on the fluffy cap with the long scarf attached, flinging the ends around her neck to dangle down her back, and jumping up to go and look at herself in the mirror.

"It's so soft!" she said, stroking it. "Now I won't have to wear that old hat of Sam's anymore!"

"Well," said Mother. "you talked so much about Patricia's that I knew you wanted one, so I got the pattern from Mrs. Rabbit."

"I can hardly wait to go back to school -- with this and my new dress, and the bracelet from Sam, I'll just feel beautiful all day!"

"You better worry about trying to feel smart all day," laughed Roscoe, but when no one was looking, he was also at the mirror, holding up his new sweater.

"When did you find time to do all this knitting, Mother?" asked Roberta. "You made sweaters for everyone, mittens, and hats -"

"Oh, well, you always make time for what you really want to do!"

Skitch had finally been given his packages and opened each one with exclamations of delight and surprise, but when he was finished, he returned to the bows and pine cones and ribbons.

"Next Christmas, I'm going to wrap up a whole lot of wrapping paper and give it to Skitch," said Roberta in exasperation.

While the children admired their gifts and ran to try on new clothes and place their loot in their bedrooms, Mother collected the wrappings, sorting Skitch's things from the others and surreptitiously slipping the baseball from Roscoe and the tiny penknife from Sam into her apron pocket.

They all bounded down the stairs again.

"Now sit down, we have your present, Mother, and we think you'll really like this one. We made it ourselves."

Good-humoredly, Mother seated herself again in her armchair and waited until her gift was presented to her. Recalling the children's' gift last year, she hoped that this time she would be able to guess what it was without needing an explanation. She and Father had carefully unwrapped the voluminous layers of paper to find a large mound of clay with designs tooled in it, and a tiny hole in the top.

With quick glances at each other, she and Father had raved mightily. They admired the designs, commented on the little hole, hefted it up and looked vaguely around to decide where to put it, all without having a single idea of what it was. When Roscoe told them how each had contributed to making the vase, Father and Mother Mouse vociferously renewed their exclamations of admiration while the children beamed.

But now Mother opened the package to find the large candle, and her admiration was genuine.

"Why, this is beautiful! It's the nicest present I have ever received!"

"Even better than the vase last year?" asked Roscoe with a wicked little grin.

Mother blushed.

"Father and I loved the vase. You know it still sits on Father's desk in the library, with stalks of dried lavender in it."

"What would you have done with it," asked Roscoe, "if we hadn't told you what it was? Oh, never mind, I know," he laughed. "It would have gone into the Keepsake Trunk!"

"No, no," smiled Mother, "it would have been placed somewhere in the house where everyone who came would see it and know the love that went into making it. Besides," she sighed, "our old trunk has finally seen its last days. I had to remove everything from it and place them in little boxes in my closet."

"Mother, light the candle now!" cried Roberta impatiently.

Obediently, Mother carefully took the candle to the dining room table, placing it on a pewter stand.

"There," she said, as she lit the wick, "now we can enjoy the bay scent all day. By the time the Muskrats arrive, it will have drifted throughout the house."

At the reminder, the children jumped up.

"Oh, we still have so much to do! Come on, Sarah," said Roberta, "we'll get our bedroom done together, and then you can help Mother and I'll dust and straighten the rest of the house."

The children rushed to get their chores done while

Mother cleared up the breakfast things and set about the early preparations for Christmas dinner.

By mid-afternoon, all was ready. The dinner was waiting on the stove and in the oven with the big serving dishes nearby, Roberta had set the table and removed Mother's candle to a low table by the hearth, while Sam waited impatiently by the living room window for the Muskrats to appear.

"Here they are!" he called.

Mother rushed out the front door to welcome them, the children right behind her. Seeing Joelle carrying little Talia, Mother went to help her with the burden. Roscoe escorted Father Muskrat, who was leaning heavily on his cane. Sam, Roberta and Sarah met Nick and Ned at the gate. Amidst the greetings, Mother suddenly halted.

Something was burning!

"Roscoe!" she cried in alarm, "run into the house and see if the stove is still on."

Just as he darted into the house, Mother heard Skitch uttering loud squeaks. Looking about and realizing he was not with her, she rushed back inside herself, almost running into Roscoe.

Roscoe had Skitch in his arms and thrust the still-crying baby into his mother's arms.

"Fire, Mother! Skitch was at the candle and now the tree's going up!"

He rushed back into the house and Mother, in a panic,

ran outside with Skitch, checking him over to see if he was burned.

Father Muskrat shouldered past her, continued on into the house and took the wet towel from Roscoe, who was ineffectually trying to put out the tree.

"The pail outside the door -- fill it with water -- have the others bring more in any containers you have," he said tersely, throwing the towel over the flames and snatching at the tree to pull it away from the window before the curtains took fire.

Roscoe ran to do as he was bid, yelling at Sam and his sisters to get buckets, anything, and fill them with water.

Father Muskrat continued to move anything flammable away from the tree, trying to contain the fire until Roscoe returned.

The little brigade of pails and buckets soon appeared and within a few moments they all stood, bedraggled and looking sadly at the smoking ruins of the Christmas tree.

"It was so beautiful!" whispered a stricken Sarah.

"It looks like Skitch started playing with the candle and tipped it over," said Roscoe.

"Oh, no!"

They all looked at Roberta.

"It's my fault -- I moved it because there wasn't going to be room on the table for it, and I set it low enough for him to reach it!"

"I should have kept a better eye on Skitch," said Mother, walking in with Skitch on her arm. "No one is hurt -- and that's the most important thing. Skitch got a little scorched, that's all," she smiled wanly.

"The room is a mess," said Sam, surveying the damage.

"Well, we'll soon have that to rights, won't we?" smiled Father Muskrat to the children. "Look, the tree was still quite green, so only a few branches really caught. We'll cut off the burnt ones and get them outside, and stand the tree back up. Can you bring a mop, Sarah? And Joelle and Roberta can pick up the ornaments that fell -- careful there, none are broken that I can see -- and Roscoe, take the rug out on the back porch, it's all wet. Here, Mrs. Mouse, you just sit down here with Skitch, that's right. Now, Nick and Ned, you can help me get the tree turned around so the spot with the missing branches is to the back."

The children bustled about, and Father Muskrat worked quietly and efficiently as he talked, so the room was soon put to rights. Sam was down on his hands and knees with old towels drying the floor, when Sarah came downstairs from the linen closet with another rug to place by the hearth.

Father Muskrat raised his head and sniffed the air.

"Do I smell something still burning?"

"Oh! The pie!" cried Mother, jumping up, placing Skitch in her chair and running to the kitchen. She returned a moment later, forlorn, and holding a burnt pie.

"Well," she sighed, "it's a good thing Mrs. Mole made the chocolate cake, because at least it's all right."

Dumping the pie into the metal container Roscoe had brought in for the debris, she picked up Skitch and sat down again.

"I'm so sorry, Mr. Muskrat, this is terrible for you -"

"Now don't you worry yourself about this, Mrs. Mouse. Look! Everyone is fine, no one is hurt, no real damage has been done, everything's cleaned up -"

At that very moment, the three girls were wafting dish towels dampened with lilac water throughout the rooms to take away the odors.

Father Muskrat sat down beside Mrs. Mouse and patted her arm.

"I'm just glad we were here to help," he said soothingly.

Mother looked up, still distraught.

"At first I thought that Skitch -- that Skitch -- then when I knew he was all right, and that no one was in danger, all I could think of was -- well, you may not think this is so important, but I kept thinking of all my keepsakes, all the things I've saved through the years -- from Father Mouse, from the children when they were babies -- I couldn't have gotten them out, because they're all in boxes stuffed away in corners of my closet, and if I had lost them -"

Father Muskrat could see that Mother Mouse was still in mild shock from what she had been through. He motioned Roscoe over.

"Can you get your mother a cup of tea?" At Roscoe's worried look, he added, "She's all right now, but will feel a lot better in a few minutes."

Roscoe hurried to fulfill the unaccustomed task.

Soon they were all over the excitement of the fire, and gathered together comfortably around their mother and Father Muskrat. Roberta sat on the hearth, scraping half-heartedly at a little pile of melted wax.

"At least it still smells nice," she said, and they were all able to laugh a little.

Once he saw that Mother Mouse was herself again, Father Muskrat said, "Well, I guess we're all about ready for that dinner, Mrs. Mouse. Speaking for myself, I've worked up a pretty good appetite."

She looked up and smiled, thankful for his lead in resuming their Christmas festivities.

"It will be on the table in a few minutes," she said. "Roscoe, will you seat everyone at the table? And Sarah and Roberta, you can help me carry out the serving dishes."

"It still smells a little funny," said Sarah when they were all at the table. She wrinkled her nose.

"I can't smell anything but this delicious food," said Father Muskrat, looking around at the steaming dishes, then at Mother Mouse, who smiled her thanks.

*Soon they were all over the excitement of the fire, and gathered together comfortably around their mother and Father Muskrat.*

"It sort of smells like Roberta did the cooking," said Sam, and everyone giggled.

Mother had already filled their glasses with apple cider, and nodded to Father Muskrat to give the Christmas toast.

He thought a moment, then raised his glass.

"We all have more to be thankful for than I ever realized -- dear friends, loving family, our lives, our health, our homes. Thank you," he said, looking at each of the Mouse family in turn, "for opening up your hearts and your home to us today. We'll remember this special day for the rest of our lives, for we've already experienced the magic of Christmas."

They were all silent a moment after the heartfelt words, but after their sips of cider, they broke into laughter at Sam's muttered comment.

"We'll remember this day, too."

And then the festive dinner began. There was a lot of happy and relieved chatter, for any shyness that might have remained had long since disappeared and they all felt a shared relief and exuberance after the near disaster. The children talked like old friends and Mother Mouse and Father Muskrat smiled to see the joyful faces around the table.

Before long, they were gathered around the hearth with hot chocolate, the grown-ups reminiscing about Christmases past, and the children talking about school and all the other concerns of their daily lives.

Roberta and Sarah slipped quietly from the group, Roscoe glancing up at them with a smile as they went. Turning back to the others, he chatted gaily to cover their disappearance.

A moment later, the girls returned with their arms

loaded with the wrapped gifts. They placed them on the rug in the middle of the circle of children and smiled at Joelle, Nick and Ned.

Father Muskrat looked at Mother Mouse questioningly.

"We did have a few little gifts," she murmured, "but apparently my children have expanded on our plan."

Joelle looked up at Sarah and Roberta.

"Are these all for us?" she asked hesitantly.

The Mouse children nodded.

"Hurry! Open them up!"

Nick and Ned whooped in delight and tore at the wrappings.

"Look at this, Father!"

"Ned, here's a Chutes and Ladders game!"

Their ecstatic exclamations made everyone smile.

Sam couldn't help but feel a little pang when they opened the package of marbles.

"Two purees, Nick!"

"And three cat's eyes, a pee wee and a boulder!"

Sam glanced up at Roscoe, who nodded and smiled to him. Sam grinned back.

Joelle had quietly opened her gifts and sat with the shoes, embroidered purse and knitted sweater spread out before her.

Her eyes were shining and she looked at and touched each thing with pleasure.

"Your sweater is the same pattern as mine," said Sarah. "We can wear them on the same day. We'll be like twins."

"Triplets," laughed Roberta. "Mine is that pattern, too, but we all have a different color."

"Is it all right if I put on the shoes now?" asked Joelle.

"Of course!" chorused Sarah and Roberta, and watched as Joelle slipped off her sandals.

Sarah looked at them curiously.

"Did you make them yourself, Joelle?"

Joelle blushed and tried unobtrusively to hide them.

"No, no!" said Sarah. "May I see them? Did you weave them yourself?"

"Yes," said Joelle, extending the sandals to her. "I dried the reeds and flattened them, then wove the sole and the tops. I lined them, but even with socks they're not very warm," she added with dissatisfaction.

Now wearing the little polished boots, she extended one foot slightly.

"These are so much nicer," she sighed.

Sarah was still examining the woven sandals and admiring the workmanship.

"When summer comes, would you help me make a pair of these?" she asked hesitantly.

Joelle's face glowed.

"Of course I would!"

Roberta picked up the embroidered purse.

"Isn't it lovely?" asked Joelle. "I haven't had anything this nice since -- since Mother was alive."

Roberta handed her the purse with a lump in her throat.

"I'm so glad it's yours, then," she whispered.

Sarah put her arm around Roberta's waist and gave her a hug.

"I can't begin to thank you for this," said Father Muskrat, seated with Talia on his lap and her gifts surrounding him. He had wound up the little pig, but Talia would not let go of it long enough to see it waddle about the room. Instead, she held it in her chubby paws, enchanted by the motions of its legs and the whirring noise it made.

Father Muskrat took out a large handkerchief, wiped his eyes and blew his nose.

"It's all part of the Christmas magic," said Mother Mouse softly.

Roscoe and Sam were playing a game of marbles with Nick and Ned on the dining room floor, and Sarah and Roberta had taken Joelle upstairs to show her their own

Christmas presents, when Mother heard a sound from outside.

"That sounds like -"

"Like the Beavers' pony cart," finished Father Muskrat, rising and going to the door.

Like a fresh wind, the Beavers swept through the door, laughing and chattering, their arms loaded with gifts.

The girls clammered back down the stairs to see what the commotion was about.

"Why, what's all this?" said Mother, flabbergasted.

"We heard you were having Christmas together and we couldn't let you keep all the fun to yourselves!" roared Father Beaver.

He began handing out packages right and left.

"Here, Sam! Roberta, this big one's for you and the tiny one for Sarah. Nick and Ned, yours are all in one package, and, let me see -- oh, Roscoe, for you, and here's Joelle's and Skitch's, Talia's and Mother Mouse's."

He handed the last package to Mother, who sat too dumbfounded to speak.

The Beaver children hung around excitedly as the presents were opened, chattering, explaining, demonstrating. Mother Beaver sat down in the chair Father Muskrat had offered to her and fell into deep discussion with Mother Mouse.

Father Beaver motioned to Father Muskrat.

"Thought I'd just check to see if you had a little time on your hands, Muskrat," said Father Beaver.

"Nothing but time, I'm afraid."

"Well, I know you usually build houses, but would you be willing to work on smaller things -- like furniture? Mother's been after me to get a new buffet for the dining room, and our wood chairs need new rush seats and tightening of the joints -"

"I would most certainly be willing to!" responded Father Muskrat in a daze.

"Then," went on Mr. Beaver, "I know old Mole has a commission or two he'd like to talk to you about -- he doesn't have much time at home to keep up with everything, you know."

"This is wonderful," stammered Father Muskrat. "But whatever gave you the idea of approaching me?"

He looked at Father Beaver with some suspicion.

"You wouldn't have created these jobs now, would you? I most definitely want the work, but I don't want my neighbors feeling they have to come up with 'jobs' for me."

"Oh, no," said Father Beaver hastily. "We've needed someone around here for a long time who could do this kind of work -- we'd never thought of coming to you before because we didn't think it was quite in your line, but someone encouraged us to talk to you."

Father Beaver nodded towards Mother Mouse.

Father Muskrat looked over to where Mother Mouse and Mother Beaver were chatting companionably.

"I have a lot to thank her for," was all he managed to say.

"All right, all right! Time to load up and say our good-byes!" called Father Beaver.

"Come on," said Thad. "You Muskrats are going back with us in the cart!"

While Sarah and Roberta helped the Muskrat children bundle up their gifts, Mother Mouse and Roscoe quickly packaged up the jars of preserves and canned vegetables and fruits in a large basket.

Sam was told to watch Skitch and Talia, and "Don't let them get into anything," cautioned Mother.

Good-byes and thank-yous were heartily exchanged as the Muskrats and the Beavers loaded up the cart and took their seats, the children jumbled helter-skelter in the back, everyone tucked in with heavy warm blankets.

Father Muskrat took Mother Mouse's hand at the door and pressed it firmly.

"Not only the best of neighbors, but a good friend as well," he said quietly.

The cart trundled down the road, the Mouse family clustered in the doorway waving and calling out final farewells.

Then the cart and its waving passengers disappeared over a little rise and they made their way back inside and closed the door against the cold night air.

"Oh, Mother," sighed Roberta, "I am so happy!"

"So am I," echoed Sarah, "but I'm so tired, too!"

"Yes," said Mother, glancing at the tree, "it's been a rather -- hectic day, hasn't it?"

"Do you know Joelle does extra studies at home?" asked Roscoe in a reflective tone as he gazed at the fire. "She wants to go to school in town after she finishes here in the village and doesn't know whether or not they'll be able to afford it. She does all this extra work in addition to everything else she does at home just so she'll be ready in case she can."

"And she told me the reason they all eat their lunch separately is because they didn't have enough to share with anyone else, and didn't want us making fun of them," said Sarah in a low voice.

There was a little silence and then Sam spoke.

"You know, watching Nick and Ned so happy with my old toys made me feel funny. I mean, I always thought we were kind of poor, but I guess I didn't realize how much we really have."

There were murmurs of agreement.

"I think," said Mother quietly, "that no matter what we may lack in material things, there's something in which all of us are very rich."

They waited expectantly.

"Loving kindness," said Mother. "And that's the true magic of Christmas."

# X - SAM'S GROUNDED

At home Sam would spend a lot of time in his room reading. He quoted from books and used big words that none of the others understood, and he was always finished with his homework while the others were still struggling with theirs.

When Robbie Hedgehog told him of his home run, Sam looked at him blankly. After all, baseball was a pleasant pastime, but not something to get so excited about! When the other boys were discussing fishing and camping trips and exchanging trading cards of sports heroes, Sam would get bored and drift away. On those occasions he would find a quiet corner, breathe a sigh of relief, and settle down to read.

He accepted Wally Mole, even though he thought Wally was dull, partly because Wally lived right next door, partly because Sam basked in the worshipful looks Wally bestowed on him. He could always count on a willing audience in Wally when he wanted to rhapsodize over a new book or a poem.

Yes, Wally was always handy when he needed him. But sometimes he was just a little in the way.

"I'm sorry, Wally, you'd better run on and play with the others," said Sam.

Sam glanced at his classmates, Franklin Beaver and Mickey Squirrel. "We're going to be working on something and I don't think you'll really understand it, you see, because you haven't gotten that far in math yet."

"Oh, okay, Sam," said Wally, somewhat mortified, for he had followed Sam around the first part of the noon recess in the enjoyment of being with him, and a bit proud that he had been accepted by the group. He had been content to just listen to them talking, unable to contribute, not completely following the discussion, but, as always, a willing and attentive listener.

Feeling a slight twinge of conscience, Sam patted him on the shoulder. "See, it's just some problems the others are having with quadratic equations, and I need to give all my attention to that. You'd probably have more fun playing with the others."

Sam turned quickly away as Wally looked up at him with his little eyes blinking and shiny.

"Sure, Sam," he said.

"Come on, guys," said Sam to the others. He trudged ahead without looking back, because he knew he would see Wally standing there with that sad little smile.

"Hey, slow down, Sam!" called Franklin. "Where are you going, anyway?"

"Sorry," muttered Sam.

"Look," said Mickey, "Why don't we go on up the hill? We can have some peace and quiet there and no one will bother us."

Franklin looked disapproving. "I don't think we'd better. You know we're not really supposed to -- there's a lot of old mine shafts there."

Mickey laughed. "They've been filled in for ages and ages."

Sam looked uncertainly from Franklin to Mickey. "You know, we've never actually been told we can't -"

"See?" said Mickey. "They've been warning us about that for years and nothing's ever happened. I think they just don't want the little ones playing up there."

Mickey strode on ahead, leading the way. With some misgivings, Sam and Franklin followed him.

"Now, what did I tell you?" said Mickey as he stood on the top of the slight rise and looked around him.

"Well," said Franklin, "It's a little wet up here. It's all that rain." He looked longingly down the hillside.

"Oh, come on," said Sam, "We're here now. Let's get

to work."

Sam walked a short distance away, seeking a dry spot in which to sit and work.

Suddenly there was a sharp cry!

Franklin and Mickey, startled, turned, but couldn't see Sam.

"Sam, where are you?" called Franklin.

There was no response. Franklin and Mickey looked at each other.

"Do you think he's playing a game?" asked Mickey a bit fearfully.

"No. Not Sam."

"Where could he have gone? There's nowhere to hide!"

The two boys surveyed the rounded hilltop in bewilderment.

"Mickey!" came a faint cry from behind them and the boys whirled.

"Careful!" warned Franklin.

Holding his arm out in front of Mickey to keep him from rushing forward, Franklin slowly walked across the grass, testing the ground carefully before each step. Then he stopped.

"There!" he breathed.

In front of the boys, almost hidden by the grass, was a

deep indentation in the earth. The ground was soggy and soft and Franklin slowly and deliberately backed up, drawing Mickey with him.

"Sam?" he called.

Sam's voice came, mournful and hollow sounding.

"I'm here, down in the hole."

"Are you okay? Are you hurt?"

"No. No, I don't think so. It's just muddy and dark. I tried to climb out but I can't."

"Don't try any more," said Franklin hastily. "I think it's one of the old shafts. Don't try to climb, Sam, okay? You might cause the sides to cave in."

There was silence for a moment, then Sam's voice came quietly. "Okay. I'm not going to move."

Franklin's mind was a-whirl. What should he do? They didn't dare go closer to the shaft, for if the earth collapsed around it, they would all be trapped, and -- and -- Sam was already down there. The mud could slide right on top of him.

For an instant panic overtook him. He turned to run down the hill.

Then he stopped. He couldn't leave Sam alone.

"Mickey," he commanded, "Go down and tell Mrs. Givens what's happened. She'll know what to do. I'll stay here with Sam."

Without a word Mickey took off down the hill,

slipping and sliding in the wet grass. His heart almost stopped when his foot sunk in a muddy spot he hadn't seen. Was it another mineshaft? How frightening! But the ground held and he flew on.

A moment later he was in the doorway of the schoolroom, gasping for breath. Mrs. Givens looked up at him, prepared to chastise the boys for not listening for the bell and for returning late from recess, but stopped when she saw Mickey's face.

"What is it?" she said, a sudden cold fear clutching her.

"Sam!" said Mickey, still trying to catch his breath. He could see the faces turned to him, the other children wide-eyed. One student leapt up and strode quickly toward him.

"What about Sam?" asked Roscoe, taking Mickey by the arm. "Where is Sam?

"Mine shaft," he gasped.

Before anyone could stop him, Roscoe was out the door and headed for the hill. Mrs. Givens rushed after him.

"Roscoe! Roscoe! Come back! You can't help, you might make it worse. We've got to get the men, some rope, boards -- you can't just go up there walking around."

Mrs. Givens held her breath as she watched Roscoe's face. She saw him struggle with himself and look back up the hill. She couldn't stop him if he was determined to go, but it was so dangerous!

She took a deep breath when Roscoe retraced his steps,

and moved to meet him.

"Look, Roscoe," she said quietly and as calmly as she could, "I need help. Someone must go get the men and get Mr. Rabbit at the store to bring ropes, a basket. And we need boards. They'll know what else. And someone has to stay with the smaller children, keep them in the classroom. I need someone older, someone steady to do that." She looked at Roscoe, who glanced back up the hill.

"Mrs. Givens," came a quiet voice, and she looked down to see Wally Mole beside her.

"Someone should be with Sam," said Wally. "Someone needs to let him know that help is coming, and keep talking to him and stuff, because as long as he's talking, we know he's okay, you see."

"Franklin's there!" said Mickey.

Wally looked at him, then again to Mrs. Givens, and spoke softly. "Franklin's too heavy, Mrs. Givens. Someone light should take a board, put it on the ground, then lie down and ease out on it, so they spread out their weight."

"Yes, yes, I see," said Ms. Givens. "Do you think Mickey could do that?" She did not feel at all odd asking Wally for advice.

Wally wrinkled his brow. "No, still too heavy." He looked up. "Maybe you, Mrs. Givens? Mickey could go into the village now, and Roscoe can stay in the classroom."

Before Mrs. Givens could give him the order to go,

Mickey had dashed off, running as if his life -- or Sam's -- depended on it.

"I think Wally's right, Mrs. Givens. I'll get one of the boards from around back and help you up the hill with it," said Roscoe.

"No, no, Wally and I can carry it. The children are still inside-"

She turned to see a quiet and fearful group huddled in the doorway.

Mrs. Givens managed a slight smile. "Okay, children," she called. "Back inside, please! Wally and I have to take care of something, and Roscoe is going to stay with you. I want you to do whatever he tells you."

Mrs. Givens and Wally started up the hill, each holding an end of the board. They were met halfway by Franklin, for whom the waiting minutes had seemed like hours. After explaining to Sam, he had hastened down the hill to see what was holding up the assistance he so desperately awaited.

"Thank you, Wally," panted Mrs. Givens as Franklin relieved them of the board and began the climb back up. "You go on back down with the others now," she smiled.

Wally was more than willing to do so. He had an idea and wanted to at least follow through with it to see if what he thought he had seen was what he actually had seen.

Barely nodding to Mrs. Givens, Wally hastened down the hill, mounted the schoolhouse steps and paused in the shadows of the entryway. He could hear Roscoe and the children. They were playing hangman, two games at once it looked like -- a simple one with "cat" or "ball" for the younger children, and longer words for the older ones. Satisfied that no one knew he was there, Wally went to work.

Cupboards, shelves and coat hooks lined the walls of the cloakroom. Wally headed for the bookcase with the two lower doors that he had explored one rainy day, and in which he had found, among the cobwebs and dust accumulated over a period of years, old ledgers and documents -- village records. They had been stored here apparently because there was nowhere else to keep them. Wally had leafed through the pages, intrigued by the messages from many years ago, the references to the grandparents and great-grandparents of his schoolmates. There were records about land sales and marriages and births and deaths, about the building of the school house, about crops, and, most importantly, about the mine.

He recalled glancing curiously at the old maps and now hunted feverishly through the volumes.

Where were they? The titles to the ledgers were faded and illegible. Why hadn't he thought to notice before which one they were in?

Could someone have taken it out? No. No one looked at these old volumes. They had been stored here for years before Wally found them.

Here it was!

Wally paused for a moment.

Even if he was lucky enough to find what he was looking for, and could decipher it, did he have the courage to go through with it?

And then he found exactly what he was looking for. The old mine maps, showing where all the shafts, now filled in and forgotten, had been located.

But it was frustrating! The school hadn't even been built when the maps had been made, so he had to use the road and the village as landmarks. Yes, there was the gently rolling hill, there the stream, there was where the school would be built.

And there was the shaft in which Sam had fallen.

Wally carefully studied the map. He had to be very, very sure before he went ahead. He was haunted by Mrs. Givens' last words as she followed Franklin up the hill: "Oh, Wally, if only your father were here..."

Trying to fix it all in his head, he finally, with exasperation and some little guilt, tore the page from the ledger and slipped out of the building.

Wally stood at the foot of the hill and got his bearings. Yes, that had to be the shaft. Approaching the small rise, he could hear Mrs. Givens' soft voice and, fainter still, Sam's responses. She looked up as Wally stopped a little distance away, afraid to walk closer.

"Oh, Wally, what's taking them so long?"

"I suppose it's because Mickey had to get there first,

then they'd have to get the stuff..." His voice trailed off as he heard Sam.

"Mrs. Givens? Mrs. Givens!"

"Yes, Sam, I'm still here!"

"Mrs. Givens, there's more water." He sounded more puzzled than afraid, but it was all Wally needed to hear. He descended the rise, circled and climbed up well beyond where Sam was. Bushes and tall grass, green and lush with the winter floods, hid him from his teacher. Was he too far away? She seemed so small, and he couldn't even hear her voice still comforting Sam.

Wally stopped again and looked at the map, at the hill, and at Mrs. Givens. He would have to tunnel down at an angle to meet the shaft Sam was in. If he ended up too deep, he would be in water himself; too shallow, and his tunnel would meet the shaft too high to help Sam -- and he might cause the walls to collapse.

And then he could see it in his mind. He could see it as clearly as Sam saw the solution to an algebra problem, or the complexity of plot and theme in a book.

He would begin his tunnel right there, go at that angle, and he should meet the shaft at a height to which Sam could climb.

If only he didn't encounter water!

Wally took not another moment to think, but immediately knelt in the tall grass and began to burrow in the soil. It was damp and dark and earth-smelling. The urgency of his work made his little paws fly, and Sam's last words echoed in his mind again and again, "...there's more water!"

*It was damp and dark and earth-smelling. The urgency of his work made his little paws fly.*

"Where are they?" thought Mrs. Givens frantically, even as she answered Sam in a calm and soothing tone.

Then she heard voices and looked around carefully.

There they were! Carrying rope and a basket and boards to lay around the shaft to allow them to approach.

"Sam!" she cried joyfully, "they're here! Do you hear me? The men are here!"

There was no response from Sam.

Dared she inch further ahead on the board to peer down the shaft? No, she would wait until the others came. They would know better what to do.

"Sam?" she called again. Still no response.

And then she saw Mr. Beaver, Mr. Rabbit and Mr. Hedgehog. They had begun to mount the small rise, but had now paused and were looking at the ground.

It's wet, she thought, and they're trying to figure out the best way to approach.

Slowly she slid backwards on the board, onto the grass and away from the shaft, careful to keep her weight spread over as large an area as possible. When she was sure it was safe, she stood and waved.

"Here! He's up here! But he's not answering anymore! Hurry!"

Mr. Beaver began to ascend, but Mr. Hedgehog grabbed his arm and shook his head. Then he waved his hand in a wide circle and discussed something with Mr.

Rabbit. Finally, they motioned Mrs. Givens to come down to them.

"What? What is it? We've got to hurry!" she said breathlessly as she joined the group.

"We can't rush it, Mrs. Givens," said Mr. Rabbit calmly. "We've got to find the driest ground and approach from that angle."

"Look, I can go back up -- it holds me. Give me the rope and the basket!"

"No, Mrs. Givens," said Mr. Beaver solemnly. "It will hold you, but when you start hauling Sam out of there, the sides are going to go. We really need two men up there -- one could do it in a pinch, but he'd have to be standing right over the shaft, which would mean a lot of weight right on the weakest spot -- the edge."

"But we've got to do something!" she cried, looking from one to the other.

"Yes, yes, we know, and that's what we're planning," said Mr. Hedgehog soothingly.

Mrs. Givens closed her eyes briefly, and let the men continue their discussion. They were right, of course. They couldn't just go rushing up there with all good intentions. That would be as bad as doing nothing at all, for they could not afford to cause a cave-in.

"It's just that he's not answering anymore," she whispered.

But the men had not heard her. They were already

advancing around the rise and beginning to lay boards.

It seemed to go painfully slowly.

One would edge out and lay a board, while another came behind, pushing a board ahead of him. The closer to the mineshaft they came, the slower it seemed to go. She continued to watch them, oblivious to everything else.

There, they were almost to the shaft.

No, Mr. Beaver was waving them back. Another board -- they had to circle it, lay boards around it. Would they ever get to the shaft itself?

Discussion ensued among the men and they felt hope slipping away. They couldn't approach the shaft without serious likelihood of a cave-in. Would they be too late to save Sam? How could they face Mrs. Givens and the other children?

Worse still, how would they face Mother Mouse?

Mrs. Givens was also quickly losing all hope of saving Sam. She was so absorbed in watching the men, now frozen in despair, that she did not hear the voice behind her.

"Mrs. Givens?"

Wally cleared his throat and spoke more loudly than he intended. "Mrs. Givens!"

Mrs. Givens turned.

She let out a little scream.

Standing before her were two large clods of mud. One of them spoke,

"Mrs. Givens?"

For a moment she was certain that she was going to faint.

Then, with sudden clarity, she realized it was Wally and Sam!

She grabbed them both in her arms, unmindful of the mud and water, and yelled up the hill.

"They're safe! Sam's here!"

The figures near the shaft looked up at her voice. She released Wally and waved one arm, beckoning them to come down. The men descended the hill quickly when they saw the three muddy figures.

"He's here, he's safe! He's out of the shaft!"

They crowded around Sam, wiping the mud from him as if to assure themselves that it was Sam, that he was not still in the shaft.

"Thank goodness! I don't know what you boys were doing up there -- don't you know how dangerous it is?" said Mr. Beaver, the concern and relief obvious in his voice.

"We've been talking about fencing this off for years now," said Mr. Hedgehog. "I guess it's about time we got around to it."

Mrs. Givens had run ahead to the school and returned,

the children trailing her. Roscoe rushed up to Sam and stopped short.

"Boy, you are really going to be in trouble!" he said.

Then he hugged Sam as hard as he could.

Mr. Hedgehog and Mr. Rabbit had walked halfway up the hill, planning the weekend's work -- fencing off the mine shaft area and posting warning signs. Mr. Beaver and Mrs. Givens were still hovering over Sam now that they had extricated him from Roscoe's clutch and all were talking at once, telling what had happened, how awful it had been, laughing in relief that Sam was safe.

"Where's Wally?" asked Sam.

"What, Sam?" said Mrs. Givens at the interruption.

"Where's Wally? He got me out."

"He got you out?" She seemed stupefied and looked at Mr. Beaver, who just shrugged, mystified.

"Where is he?" Sam asked again, looking around the yard.

"There he is," said Roscoe. "He's at the pump."

They walked over as a group to where Wally was doing his best to remove the mud, which was quickly drying in his fur. He looked up as they approached, blinking and shaking his head to get the water out of his eyes.

"Mother will kill me if she sees me this dirty," he murmured.

"How did he get you out?" asked Mr. Beaver with curiosity.

"I don't know," said Sam. "Just, the water was coming up higher and higher, then all of a sudden there was this big plop and dirt and mud fell in, and I thought the shaft was caving in, but it was Wally. And he helped me climb up to where he was and we crawled through this tunnel." He shuddered. "It was dark and wet and muddy and Wally kept saying, "It's okay, just a little further, we're almost there", and then, we were. We were out. And he led me down the back of the hill and then we found Mrs. Givens..." his voice trailed off and he looked from Mr. Beaver to Mrs. Givens. "Wally saved my life."

Mr. Beaver turned away for a moment, then knelt down by Wally.

"Well," he said gruffly, "You really did well, Wally. You really did well." Furtively, he wiped his hand across his eyes. "Let's get this mud off the two of you and get you inside."

"Oh, yes," said Mrs. Givens, bustling about. "Thad, Homer, bring the blankets from the cloakroom."

Soon the two boys were washed and dried, wrapped in blankets and toasting themselves before the old iron stove in the classroom, with their schoolmates clustered around them.

"How did you know what to do, Wally?" asked Megan.

"Well, I just remembered the old books in the

cloakroom, and that somewhere in there were maps of the mine and the shafts and that. Then I found them, and I went up and tunneled in."

"He 'found a map,' he 'went up and tunneled'," murmured Mr. Beaver to himself.

Mrs. Givens regarded Wally in silent amazement. "I didn't even know what was in those cupboards -- just old ledgers and records. I never would have thought to look for a map, or," she added, looking up at Mr. Beaver, "known what to do if I had found it!"

"I just remembered you saying if only my father was here," said Wally, "and I tried to think what he would do."

Mr. Beaver and Mrs. Givens drew away and talked together as the children continued to ask Wally and Sam for more details, and shuddered at the thought of Sam waiting helplessly at the bottom of the shaft, -- and then the trip through the long, wet tunnel.

"How on earth did he figure out where to start his tunnel -- then the angle -" Mr. Beaver scratched his head. "I guess I never really gave that boy the credit he deserves. Somehow I just didn't think he was that smart," he said apologetically.

Mrs. Givens smiled faintly. "There are many ways to be smart, aren't there, Mr. Beaver. I think a lot of us underestimated him," she said, looking to where Wally was surrounded by his admiring friends, and modestly answering their excited questions.

Sam had withdrawn a little from the group, and Mrs.

Givens walked over to sit beside him.

"Well, I'm glad everything's turned out so well. Do you feel all right, Sam?"

He smiled and gestured toward the chattering group of children. "Yes, I'm fine, Mrs. Givens, thanks to Wally."

"Wally's getting a lot of attention, right now, Sam. I'm sure if you joined the group, they would like to hear you tell them what happened." She watched him closely.

"It's okay. Wally can tell them. After all, he's the one who actually did something. All I did was fall down a hole."

"Sam -" began Mrs. Givens.

Sam looked up at her with a smile on his face. "Mrs. Givens, you know it's true. We weren't even supposed to be up there. And – and -"

Sam looked down shamefacedly.

By now his voice had sunk to a near whisper. "I wouldn't let Wally come with us because I thought he wasn't smart enough."

Mrs. Givens remained silent.

"I'm really sorry, Mrs. Givens. I deserve to just have to stay in that old hole."

Mrs. Givens smiled. "Well, hardly that, Sam, but yes, I think there might be something for all of us to learn here -- and not just about following rules."

Sam looked up at his teacher. "He's really a hero, isn't

he, Mrs. Givens? Just like in the books, a real hero."

"Yes," said Mrs. Givens as they watched Wally sitting by the stove and talking with the children, "Wally is a real, live hero."

# *XI – SOLD UP THE RIVER--AGAIN*

Baby Skitch was sulking.

Here he was again, hemmed in by those wooden slats they were always putting around him when he was outside.

He was tired of playing with that old stuffed thing. Even the wind-up box with the funny head that popped out had lost its novelty. He picked up his bottle, then threw it down. It was empty.

Earlier -- ages ago! -- he had seen his sisters leave. He had called to them, but they only turned and waved and kept on walking.

He had squealed with delight when he saw his brother Roscoe carrying his bow and arrows. Surely he would be rescued now!

But Roscoe only wiggled his fingers at Skitch and ran out the back gate. Skitch had slumped in despair.

He had followed the progress of an ant across the paving stones until that, too, had paled.

Finally, in desperation, Skitch raised his voice.

"Ma-ma! Ma-ma!"

But Mama was in the house and didn't hear him. He stood up against the slats and shook them in frustration.

He stopped in amazement. Instead of holding firmly as usual, they waggled back and forth.

Well, at least this was something new, if not all that amusing.

Skitch continued to move the slatted wood frame back and forth. Quickly growing bored, he stuck a thumb in his mouth, still rocking the frame absently with one hand.

Crash!

The thumb popped out and Skitch stared open-mouthed at the frame lying on the ground.

It took a moment for the implications of this to register in Skitch's little mind. He took one tentative step forward and looked around.

No one called out to him.

No one came and swooped him up.

In fact, as far as he could see, there was no one around

at all.

Carefully he climbed over the prostrate frame on all fours, then stood and surveyed his horizons.

With a sense of urgency he scampered around the side of the house and out to the front yard. Through the open gate lay the path to adventure!

Soon he was marching, a small lone figure, down the dusty lane.

At first he enjoyed simply basking in the unaccustomed freedom, but then slowed his walk to think. Screwing up his face, Skitch tried to bring back a memory from the long distant past.

Then his face cleared as he remembered. This was the way Roscoe had taken him when they went on the water! What fun! Too bad Roscoe wasn't here, but he could find the way himself -- just follow the road, then slide down the mud and climb on the boat in the water. He was good at climbing.

It was a much warmer day today. He wouldn't even mind if the water did come up over his toes!

Trudging on under the warm sun, Skitch was becoming disheartened. It was so far! But then he spied a glimmer of silver ahead and toddled on faster.

Yes! It was the water!

Standing on the high grassy bank, Skitch looked around in confusion.

Where was the boat?

He looked up and down the stream, craning his neck, but it was not in sight.

Only grass and trees with branches drooping into the water's edge, and -- and -- there it was!

Well, it was smaller than Roscoe's boat. Maybe it was like soap and got smaller and smaller when it sat in the water.

Blithely he sat and slid down the grassy slope. It wasn't all muddy and slippery this time, so he had to scoot along in places. But that was all right -- in fact, it was kind of fun.

He reached the boat -- an old board caught in the rushes at the water's edge, one end swaying back and forth as the current tried to shove it downstream.

Just my size, thought Skitch with satisfaction, like in the Three Bears.

Gingerly he waded into the water and plopped onto the board.

Wait -- he'd forgotten something. The stick -- Roscoe had a big stick!

Oh, well, too late now, he thought, as the board turned and drifted out towards the middle of the stream.

The water had subsided considerably since the earlier Spring rains and the current was slow and steady. For a while Skitch floated on with a satisfied grin.

Yo ho ho, he thought, I have to sit still.

Obedient to the inner command, he sat with his paws on the board at either side, looking straight ahead, only moving his eyes to see from side to side.

Rocks and weeds in the stream disrupted the flow of the sluggish current. Inevitably, Skitch was caught in a small whirlpool and his smooth ride became sudden and swift.

His board swirled quickly and was suddenly flung free!

What was happening? Where was his boat?

Skitch had hardly a moment to see it bobbing on downstream and to realize he was in the water before his head went under.

Flailing with his little paws, he surfaced once more.

"Ma-ma!" he managed to choke out before his head went under once again.

This time it did not rise to the surface, and the stream meandered peacefully on its way, the board now far downstream, twisting and turning in the water, minus its little passenger.

Startled, Father Beaver dropped his sandwich and stood up, shading his eyes as he looked towards the stream.

"Was that little Skitch Mouse I saw out there?" he

asked in astonishment.

"Oh, it couldn't have been," laughed Mother Beaver as she brushed the grass off Father's sandwich. "What on earth would he be doing out there? He's much too small to be on the river by himself!"

Father Beaver sat down reluctantly.

"Well, it sure looked like him. He was just moving along on top of the water."

Mother Beaver laughed heartily. "Here, you'd better have a glass of lemonade. Our first picnic, the first really warm day and the sun's gotten to you already."

Father took the glass and drank slowly, his eyes searching downstream for the small figure he still pictured in his mind.

There was Molly running along the bank -- she'd better be careful. I've told her, thought Father Beaver, not to run on the edge like that -- it's too slippery.

Behind her came her two brothers, right on the edge of the bank as well.

Exasperated, Father Beaver stood and motioned them to move farther up the bank. His lips tightened grimly as Molly and Thaddeus kept on coming, waving their arms wildly. They weren't paying any attention to him at all! And where did Franklin go? He must have turned and gone back downstream.

Sighing, he strode towards the oncoming children, who stopped short when they saw him approach.

"What?" called Father Beaver as he heard their faint shouts. "What did you say? Skitch? Skitch!"

Suddenly Father Beaver was all energy.

"I knew I saw the little fellow -- I knew it."

Breaking into a run, he quickly caught up to a breathless Molly, but hardly paused.

"It's Skitch," gasped Molly, "he's on the river -- all by himself!"

She stood a moment longer to catch her breath, then sped on to where her mother was gathering up the picnic remains.

Mother Beaver rose as Molly swept in.

"What is it, Molly?"

"Skitch, Mother, on the water!"

"Oh, my heavens!" breathed Mother Beaver.

Forgetting the picnic things altogether, Mother Beaver hastened after Molly, who had run back to her brother.

"Thaddeus!" she panted, "Run and hitch up the pony cart. Oh, I hope we're in time!"

Molly stood frozen in her tracks by the expression she had seen on her mother's face.

But the fear held her for only a moment. Then she thought of Father's burly figure sprinting down the path. The last she had seen of him, he was plunging down the bank before the stream went out of sight behind a curve.

Father Beaver dove into the water.

Make better time this way, he thought fleetingly.

Raising his head for just a second to look for the small figure, he shook water from his fur in bewilderment.

Where had he gone?

In the distance he saw the board turning end over end.

He's under, then, thought Father grimly as he dove again.

How murky it was at the stream's bottom! Weeds and old tree branches slowed him down, but Father sped through the water, keeping his sharp eyes open.

There! What was that?

Father Beaver turned over in the water and went back the way he had come, eyes sweeping the area below him. Suddenly he gave a powerful lunge with his broad tail and hovered over a small hump on the river bottom.

Got him! thought Father as he grabbed the back of Skitch's shirt.

With one mighty thrust, he was bobbing on top of the water, gasping for air, but holding little Skitch's head up.

He paddled quickly to shore where he saw Mother, Molly and Thad waiting with the pony cart.

A coldness enclosed Father Beaver's heart. The little form was so limp!

As soon as his feet touched bottom, he slogged

through the reeds and grasses, holding Skitch up for Mother to take and wrap in the waiting blanket.

A moment later they were all bending over him.

"He's not breathing," said Mother in alarm.

"Let's get him in the wagon. I'll continue to work on him while Thad drives to Dr. Raccoon's."

"I've sent Franklin for Mrs. Mouse," said Mother, with a catch in her voice, as Father Beaver leapt into the cart along side of Skitch.

"It's not over yet, Mother," was all he said and turned to the little bundle in the blanket as the cart lurched and Thaddeus began the wild dash to town.

Roscoe had had a most satisfying day, and now he was hungry.

Walking in the front door, he called out "Where's dinner?" but halted when he saw Sarah's and Roberta's faces.

"What's wrong?"

Sarah began to cry and Roscoe looked at her in consternation.

"Roberta?" He turned to his other sister with a puzzled look.

"It's Skitch. We think he -- maybe -- he was on the river -- we don't know how -"

"He might be drowned."

Roscoe whirled to see Sam at the foot of the staircase. He seemed calm and his voice was low and measured, but Roscoe noticed that his glasses were askew and it looked as if he had been clutching the fur on his head.

"Wha-? How?" Roscoe was dumbfounded.

"Oh, Roscoe," cried Sarah, "Franklin Beaver came to get Mother and said Skitch was out on the stream on a board, and how he ever did that I don't know, I don't even know how he got out of the backyard, but somehow he knocked over the gate -"

"Sarah!" Roscoe's voice cut through her babble and she stopped.

"How is he, Sarah? Is he all right?"

"We don't know, Roscoe, we just have to wait until Mother comes back," said Roberta in a low voice.

Roscoe's mind was a-whirl. The stream, the raft, that day with Skitch -

"Why weren't you watching him?" he demanded of his sisters.

Roberta simply looked at him with swollen, reddened eyes. Sarah appeared consumed with guilt.

"I'm sorry, I'm sorry," he said faintly, feeling dizzy. "It's not your fault."

Roscoe slumped in a dining room chair.

After a moment, Roberta asked listlessly, "Where did

Sam go?"

Her gaze wandered to the staircase and she slowly walked over and mounted the steps. Roscoe could hear the murmur of voices from upstairs, but his concentration was turned inward.

He felt cold and strange. Surely nothing could happen to Skitch! There was a lump in his throat and it felt hard to swallow. But much worse was the voice in his mind. "If only you hadn't taken Skitch out that day -- if only you'd stayed home and dug the vegetable bed – if only – if only."

"Sam's in his room," said Roberta in a lackluster voice. "He's finishing the truck he promised Skitch last month. He says," and here her voice broke, "he says he has to finish it for Skitch for when he comes home."

Roscoe was numb. Nothing felt real because none of this happened to them. Sure, sometimes a skinned knee or stubbed toe, once even a broken arm, but not -

Then he remembered when he had felt totally empty and helpless like this before -- when Daddy had died saving him.

Roscoe couldn't help but relive those terrible hours. He had stayed out too late -- he and his friends had been sledding on the hill by the woods -- and the winter storm had struck quickly and furiously. Lost and disoriented, his last memory until his father had found him was of getting sleepier and sleepier. He had been half buried in the snow when Father, who had been out searching for hours, stumbled across him, then carried him home. Roscoe was soon up and well, but Father could not recover from the prolonged exposure. His family, along with Dr. Raccoon, were by his bedside right up to the end.

Was Roscoe now going to be responsible for the loss of Skitch, just as he felt responsible for the loss of his Father? There was no way he could bear such a terrible burden!

But Roscoe had to push those anguished thoughts from his mind.

As if in a dream, he rose and said, "There's nothing we can do right now to help Skitch -- Mother's taking care of that, but we can help by getting things ready for when Mother -- and -- and -- Skitch -- get back."

Sarah looked up with wet eyes, but almost smiled with relief. It was good to have Roscoe here and to have him take charge.

"Mother had already started dinner," she began tentatively, "I -"

"Good," said Roscoe briskly. "If you can finish off in the kitchen, and you" nodding to Roberta, "can get the table set and everything else ready, I'll get the wood and start a fire in the fireplace."

At Roberta's puzzled look, he answered, "I'm cold -- I mean it's cold. By the time Mother and Skitch get back it will be chilly and I want the house warmed up for them."

Glancing at the stairs, Roberta asked, "What about Sam?"

"Leave him be, Roberta," he said softly, "let him finish Skitch's truck."

He turned and went outside to get the firewood.

Within a half-hour, the food was warming on the back of the stove. The table was laid for dinner, and a brisk fire was crackling in the fireplace.

"I turned down Skitch's bed and put out his pajamas," said Roberta.

Roscoe nodded.

The four of them sat now in the dining room, with nothing left to do but wait. Sam had silently joined them, carrying the wooden truck. He sat, fiddling with the back wheels, muttering to himself.

"The sun is going down," said Sarah to no one in particular.

Roscoe rose from his chair impetuously.

"I can't just sit and wait!" he exclaimed. "I'm going to go outside -"

"Hush!" said Sam.

There was a moment of silence and then they all heard it -- the clop-clop of Mr. Beaver's pony cart.

There was a mad rush to the door, but Roscoe held back with sudden dread.

"It's Mr. Beaver!" cried Roberta.

"I see Mother! Mother's sitting beside him, Roberta!"

"That's not Mother!"

"Yes, it is! She's got on her long cape with the hood!"

As the cart drew up to the gate, Roscoe could hear their cries as they ran to meet it.

"Mother, Mother, is Skitch okay?"

Roscoe still stood in the dining room as he strained to hear Mother's murmured response and Mr. Beaver's voice as he escorted her to the door.

Mother walked in, alone, wrapped in her voluminous cape.

Roscoe stared at her wild-eyed.

"Skitch?" he croaked.

Mother smiled tiredly.

"Right here," she said, unfolding her cloak.

Out poked a little head, beady eyes squinting in the sudden light. At Skitch's squeek, the children clustered around their mother, patting the baby, kissing him, touching him.

"Be careful, children," warned Mother, "he's still very weak."

What a bad scare they had had!

How brave of Mr. Beaver!

There were self-recriminations and promises to mind Skitch and baby-sit him well into adulthood. Sam grinned with delight as Baby grabbed the truck, spun the wheels, and cried, "Voom-voom!"

They laughed and prattled and finally moved en masse to Mother's big armchair, into which she sunk with relief.

*"Right here," she said, unfolding her cloak. Out poked a little head...*

Cradled in her lap, Skitch was the center of attention, the

focus of all eyes. They couldn't leave him, felt comfort in just seeing him there, chattering in his own little language, turning now to one favored sister, patting the other's cheek, grinning delightedly at Sam as the giver of wonderful gifts. All of it helped to banish from their minds the frightful hours before his homecoming.

Except for Roscoe.

Once he knew that Skitch was all right, the numbness once again left him. He felt pain so sudden and sharp he actually looked down at himself to see if he were injured. In the midst of the family reunion he slipped unnoticed up the stairs.

"See, Mother," laughed a gay little Sarah, "we have dinner all ready and a fire going, and here's Roberta now with a nice hot cup of tea for you, and Skitch's bed is all warm and his covers turned back, and" she paused to survey the room, "and -- everything!"

Mother murmured her gratitude.

"It was all Roscoe," chattered on Sarah. "We didn't know what to do and Roscoe came home and told us to finish dinner and set the table, and -"

"Where is Roscoe?" inquired Mother.

They all looked about, as if he might have hidden himself under the table or a chair.

"I think he went upstairs," said Sam, still enthralled by the scene of Skitch playing with the truck. He knew that if he got it finished, everything would be all right.

"Here, Roberta, hold Skitch for me," said Mother, and turned to mount the stairs.

She felt a mild foreboding as she approached Roscoe's closed door. Knocking hesitantly, she called his name.

At the muffled sound coming from the room, she opened the door and peeped in.

"Roscoe! What is it?" she said, stepping quickly to his bedside.

Roscoe was lying face down, holding a pillow over the back of his head. He looked out from the side as Mother knelt down.

"Nooo!" he groaned as Mother turned on his light, and burrowed his head again.

"Roscoe," said Mother with a no-nonsense air, and removing the pillow from his head, "now sit up and tell me what's wrong. From all I've heard, you've handled everything magnificently -- besides the relief of coming home to a warm house and dinner all prepared, you helped to keep the other children's minds off -- off Skitch's mishap."

Roscoe groaned again.

"Roscoe," said Mother in a softer tone, "Skitch is all right now. He swallowed a lot of water and -- well, there were some problems -- but Mr. Beaver got to him in time and Dr. Raccoon checked him over and said he was going to be "fit as a fiddle." So why don't you turn around and tell me what's bothering you."

Mother was taken aback by the remorseful, tear-stained face that turned towards her.

"Mother -- Mother, it's all my fault."

Mother Mouse was flabbergasted.

"All your fault, Roscoe! No, no, if it was anyone's fault at all, it was mine, for leaving him alone. When I went down and saw the gate down and Skitch gone, I – I -"

Mother paused and closed her eyes, briefly re-living that terrible moment. Would she ever be able to forget it, or Franklin's wild, desperate face in the doorway? She wanted to just clutch little Skitch and hold on to him tightly for a very long time.

"Now," said Mother, patting Roscoe's hand and setting aside her own dreadful recollections, "tell me what's wrong."

She waited patiently while Roscoe turned and groaned and made false starts, only to burrow once more beneath the pillow. Finally he emerged and spoke quickly in a quiet, strained voice, as if he couldn't bear the burden of silence another moment.

"Mother, Skitch went to the river because that's where I took him that day you were housecleaning -- remember? -- and you asked me to watch Skitch. I was going to go down and play on this old raft I found, so when I had to watch Skitch, I thought, well, why not take him along as crew -"

"Crew!" echoed Mother faintly.

Roscoe looked up.

"Are you okay, Mother?"

"Yes, yes, go on."

"Well, anyway," he continued, knotting and unknotting his fingers, "we went out on the raft, and sort of floated downstream until -- well, until we decided to get out."

"Is that all?" spoke Mother to Roscoe's averted face.

"No -- no -- we almost had an accident," Roscoe continued in a near whisper. "I lost the paddle and we almost sank."

Why, Roscoe wondered, had he thought he was so brave that day? Rescue little Skitch! He had almost drowned him! And look what it had led to!

Mother remained silent, and Roscoe finally got up enough courage to look up at her. She seemed to be thinking.

Finally she spoke.

"When you were younger, Roscoe, I had to keep a constant watch on you -- much more even than Skitch now. You were into everything, wandered everywhere, could climb over or under anything, I kept you at my side every moment, because I was responsible for you, you see, and for what you did. But now, as you grow up, you have to take more and more of that responsibility yourself. That," she emphasized with a nod," is a big part of what growing up is all about."

"Taking responsibility, you mean?"

"And thinking ahead to the consequences of your actions. Oh, Roscoe, it wasn't your fault that Skitch went to the river. Just as you had to be watched over when you were a baby, so does Skitch. Yes, I know he might not have thought of going to the river if you hadn't taken him, but he could just as easily have gotten into something equally dangerous."

Mother Mouse was relieved to see the heavy weight lift from Roscoe. Although Father's death had been devastating for them all, she was aware of the terrible blow it had been to Roscoe, and the guilt he continued to feel.

"And Roscoe," said Mother quietly, "Father would have been very proud of you today."

Roscoe looked at her in astonishment.

"I would never have known about your and Skitch's adventure if you hadn't told me."

"But I would have known," muttered Roscoe.

"Exactly. That's how I know you are growing up and why your father would trust you with Skitch any time and anywhere. It's why I look to you so much to help with the younger children."

"Really, Mother?" asked a transformed Roscoe.

"Really," said Mother with finality.

Roscoe jumped up.

"Well, let's go downstairs, Mother!" he cried. "I have

to welcome Skitch home!"

* * * * *

Later that night, after her children were tucked into bed and sound asleep, Mother closed up the house and climbed the stairs to her room. Then, as she had done so many times before, she retrieved the cardboard box from a drawer in her bureau, and sat down in the armchair with it in her lap. Plain and nondescript, the outside of the box gave no hint of its contents.

Removing the lid and folding back the tissue paper, Mother's eyes dimmed with tears as she removed, one by one, the items within.

Father's eyeglasses. His wedding ring and their marriage certificate.

She smiled a little at her own sentimentality when she unfolded a laundered and pressed handkerchief and found a sprig of rosemary. Rosemary -- for remembrance.

There was his old journal, too, a few blank pages still remaining. His last entry, a week before his death, characteristically, was about his children. He had expressed a slight concern about Roscoe who, wrote Father, would need "a firm and loving hand" to help him learn the self-discipline necessary to achieve his high goals. There was a deep affection expressed for his "Field Mouse" and his "House Mouse", and humorous references to Sam's predilection -- so like his own -- to spend too much of his time in his room, reading. "His voracious appetite for books will soon exhaust our own little library, but I think he is only half aware of the glories in the life around him. Perhaps his interest in nature, his collection of birds' nests and leaves and rocks, will help him with that."

He wrote detailed descriptions of Skitch's antics, his little "Tickle Mouse," and Mother recalled her own surprise when first reading the lines, how acutely he had been aware of his children -- their strengths, their weaknesses, their interests, their interactions with each other. She recognized in those lines the feeling she always had when he was still with them -- that great, loving presence among them. One of her sorrows was that Skitch's only memories of the father who loved him so much would be those of others handed down to him. But one day, she would let Skitch read these passages himself.

A small folded paper fell to the floor. Curious, she opened it and felt a sudden pang. It was the poem she had come across one day and copied because it had struck an emotional chord.

I folded up a grief today
And placed it on a shelf
Away from daily use, still yet
Too much a part of self

Does it remain to throw it out -
All softened, now, with wear,
Its crispness gone, a weary look
Replaces its lost flair.

With tissue lining every crease
And wrapped in velvet cloth,
It rests in place accessible
But safe from thief or moth.

For now and then I take it down
To see what none else sees:
The faded but still lovely threads
Of hopes and memories.

Replacing the items in the box and folding the tissue paper over them, Mother replaced the lid and sat for a moment with her own memories. She went to the bureau, opened the drawer, but closed it again. Turning to her closet, she made a small space on the high shelf, and gently placed the box upon it.

# XII - A Picnic in the Woods

"Ouch!"

"Did you prick your finger again, Sarah?" asked Mother Mouse as she was passing by her daughter.

"Oh, Mother," sighed Sarah, "I don't know if I'm going to have this finished in time or not. And if I do," she added, holding up her little paw with the thimble, "I don't know if I'll ever be able to use these fingers again."

Sighing deeply, she bent her head back over the embroidery frame and resumed her needlework.

Mother smiled.

"I'm sure it's going to be fine, Sarah, and you've plenty of time to finish. Roberta's helping me with the baking, so you can give all your time to your work."

Mother raised her head in alarm at the sound of a loud crash. "I'd better see what's going on in there," she murmured, sweeping on towards the kitchen with a mild look of apprehension on her face.

Roberta's head poked out of the kitchen door.

"It's okay, Mother. I just dropped the cake tin."

"If I'd only decided to do an outline rather than a satin stitch I would have been finished by now," muttered Sarah. "And these French knots!"

Sarah sighed as her thread broke, but she patiently snipped it off and began again.

It would be pretty when it was finished. She paused to hold up the pillow cover and was pleased with her progress. Skitch would like the butterflies and birds, and she liked the flowers. Those and Skitch's name were already finished. All she had left to complete were some leaves and the daisy centers.

Those darn French knots!

Sarah smiled. She could hear more clatter in the kitchen and Roberta's disgusted complaints. The odor of paint drifted in the window from where Sam and Roscoe were working on the wagon they had built. It was now a bright shiny red and the two boys were busy lettering Skitch's name on the side.

"Don't move, Sam! How am I supposed to get this letter straight if you keep moving the wagon?"

"Well, don't take so long! What do you think I am, a statue or something? I have to breathe, you know."

Here they all were, the day of Skitch's birthday, and

only now finishing off his presents! Roberta had crowed when she had completed hers early, but for her pains had drawn the task of helping to prepare the food for the picnic.

"All this work just so people can gobble it up!" was her typical response to cooking.

Roscoe was bringing the last of the picnic supplies around to the front when they heard Mr. Beaver's pony cart approaching. A few seconds later the cart was in sight and they all waved to Mr. and Mrs. Beaver on the front seat, and to Thaddeus, Franklin and Molly leaning over the side behind them.

Mr. Beaver dismounted, and stood scratching his head, looking from the cart to the huge pile of food hampers and other packages before him.

"Don't worry," laughed Mother Mouse, "we're going to walk to the woods. You only need to take the food and the children's gifts."

The Beaver children jumped out of the cart.

"We'll walk, too, okay, Daddy?"

"Sure," said Father Beaver, "but we can take Skitch in the cart. It might be a little too far for him and we don't want the guest of honor to fall asleep in the middle of his party!"

Mother handed up Skitch as Mr. Beaver and the boys loaded up the back of the cart, then watched a bit anxiously as Mr. Beaver called "Giddyap!," gave the reins a flick, and started off slowly down the road. The cart swayed and jolted a bit in the ruts, but nothing fell out.

"Come on, Roscoe!" yelled Thad, "I bet if we run we can get there before the cart does!"

Both boys tore off down the road.

Sam sidled up to his mother.

"You know, if those letters are crooked, it's not my fault," he complained. "Roscoe kept yelling at me and took so long -"

"Don't worry, I'm sure it will be fine," said Mother, patting his head.

Sarah smiled complacently. She had finished the pillow cover in plenty of time to iron it and wrap it in tissue paper and bright ribbon.

Roberta still appeared a bit befuddled.

"I hope the cake is all right," she muttered.

Mother laughed. "What a lot of gloomy Gus's! Everything -- food and wagon and all -- is going to be fine! It's a beautiful day, and it's going to be a lovely picnic -- that is, if we ever get there!"

Placing her wide-brimmed straw hat on her head, Mother started off briskly. After a moment, the children trotted after her, and were soon running on ahead, enjoying the warm air.

Mother Mouse gazed around her. It was a perfect day for a picnic, not too hot to enjoy the walk, and not too cool to make it unpleasant when they reached the shelter of the woods.

How kind of her neighbors to join them in celebrating Skitch's birthday! Mrs. Mole had voiced their sentiments when she had stated in an unguarded moment, "We're just so happy to have him still with us!"

But Mother had understood, for she felt exactly the same way. It was some time since Skitch's great adventure, but she still trembled at the thought of what could have happened whenever she saw the river. How harmless it looked, now that the water was down! There were places where you could actually see the riverbed, with brown sluggish water lazily pooling around the rocks and debris in the stream.

By the time Mother arrived at the picnic site, the Beaver's cart had been unloaded, cloths had been laid and food and hampers distributed among them. Skitch was passed around as if he were a plate of cookies. He received hugs and kisses and returned them freely, excited at all the attention and fuss.

Gradually, the children made their way into the woods and their voices could be heard among the trees, noisy and laughing. Mother Mouse began to help lay out the makings of the party.

"Oh, what a lovely cake!" admired Mrs. Hedgehog as Mother set out the platter.

"Actually, Roberta made it," said Mrs. Mouse proudly.

"Why, what do you know! It's hard to picture Roberta

so -- so -- domestic."

Mrs. Hedgehog and Mrs. Mouse looked at each other and laughed.

"Well, I think it will be a while before it happens again!"

"Oh, look," said Mrs. Hedgehog, turning to where Mrs. Squirrel was laying out jars and baskets and bowls on a large white cloth.

Mrs. Squirrel was just rising and dusting off her apron as they approached.

"Nut butter, nut jelly, nut pie, nut everything!" she said, waving her hand at the bounty spread before her. "And," she added with a humorous sigh, "it looks like I'll be making this stuff for the rest of my life!"

At her friends puzzled looks, Mrs. Squirrel explained. "After the county fair -"

"Where you won every prize in your category," added Mrs. Hedgehog dryly, for she had listened to Mrs. Squirrel's constant recounting of the event for days afterward.

"Yes, well, after that I received so many requests for recipes and finally Father said, why not offer your goods for sale? So I thought about it, and thought about it and thought, well, Father, for once in your life you're absolutely right!" Mr. Rabbit has agreed to sell my goods in Mr. Possum's store. He's going to have special labels printed up and everything, and -"

She paused as she saw light dawning on her friends' faces. "You see?"

"Why that's wonderful!" exclaimed Mother Mouse.

How that woman did chatter before she got to the point!

"I am so happy for you," said Mother Mouse with honest admiration.

"Well," admitted Mrs. Squirrel, "It's going to be a lot of work -"

"But just think how famous you'll be, and we'll all be able to have them whenever we want rather than relying on special occasions like this!" enthused Mrs. Hedgehog.

"Famous?" pondered Mrs. Squirrel, gazing into the branches of the tree above her, perhaps contemplating the source of endless supply for her breads and pies and jellies.

The two women wandered off, leaving Mrs. Squirrel to her plans.

"That really is wonderful," said Mother Mouse. "She is such a good cook and she enjoys it so much. I hope she does become famous!"

"Where's that boy of yours?" inquired Mr. Beaver as he broke away from the group of men talking and resting on the old logs. "I wanted to have a word with him sometime today."

"Do you mean Roscoe?" asked Mother curiously.

"Yes. I have a little business proposition for him," he

winked. Before turning away, he added, "Did you hear about old Mole?"

Mother had not heard, but knew he was at home from the mines for a few weeks. They had hardly seen Wally, she thought with a smile, and having his father home for a visit would be about the only thing that could keep him and Sarah apart.

"He won't be going back to the mines. Possum's offered him a position managing his land and crops around here, so he can stay home and spend time with his wife and that little son of his."

Mother glowed. "I'm so glad! Mrs. Mole would never have said so, but I know that they missed him terribly when he was gone!"

Still elated over the Mole family's improved situation, she sauntered over to a group gathered around Mrs. Rabbit, who appeared as if she were holding court.

Mrs. Rabbit was counting on her fingers. "Annie, Betty, Cassie, Dotty, Effie -" She paused. "Yes, that's all of them so far!"

"And what's the new one's name to be?" asked Mrs. Beaver with a grin.

"Well," said Mrs. Rabbit thoughtfully. "We've decided on Fiona if it's a girl and Frederick if it's a boy -- we keep them alphabetical, you know, just so I can keep track easier. We really would like a boy this time, since we have so many girls and I'm sure Fred would like a son."

Fred was certainly overwhelmed by women at the moment, for all the little rabbit girls had made a concerted run at their Father and were now clambering over him, pulling his ears and tickling his whiskers. Little Effie had taken his watch from his vest pocket and was absorbed in pulling and pushing the knob on the side. Cassie was checking his other pockets for any left over goodies, while Dotty perched on one of his knees and solemnly begged for a baby brother this time.

"Well, I hope so," grumbled Father Rabbit, "this house full of girls is getting just a bit too much for me!" His daughters laughed, for they knew how much they were loved.

By now the rest of the children were wandering in from the woods. They had sniffed the scent of the bountiful spread under the shade of the oak tree. Father Beaver was distracted from his group when he caught sight of Roscoe. He waved, then motioned Roscoe over, walking to meet him.

"Wanted to talk to you, Roscoe. You know, I need some extra help and I know that you've got one more session here at school before you go away to town." Father Beaver placed his hands in the pockets of his overalls. "Well, I know it's going to mean some extra expense for your mother, and I thought you'd like to earn a little to help."

"Would I!" exclaimed Roscoe delightedly. "That would be great! I'm really a good worker, Mr. Beaver," he said eagerly. "Have you talked to Mother yet? I'd need to get her permission, but I know she'd say yes."

"No, I haven't explained to her yet. I wanted to talk to you first, just to see, between us, if you'd be interested. You know, I'm responsible for keeping up the river and the streams, preventing the debris from collecting and damming the water flow, all of that." He waved offhandedly. "Now I'm going to be running a barge service as well, and extra hands are going to make a big difference."

Roscoe's eyes were shining. "I'd do my best, Mr. Beaver."

"I'm sure you would, Roscoe." Mr. Beaver paused, then continued more slowly "You know, it wouldn't be a lot of hours, but enough, enough. Don't want to interfere with school." And here Mr. Beaver looked at Roscoe from under his brows. "Or your chores. Your mother still needs your help."

"Oh, yes," replied Roscoe, "I'd make sure I stayed up with my schoolwork and the stuff at home."

"And," continued Father Beaver, "I need someone responsible, someone who doesn't take any risky chances, or daydream on the job."

"That's me, Mr. Beaver," stated Roscoe firmly, "now!" he added quickly, as he looked at Father Beaver with gratitude.

Roscoe's mind jumped ahead to when he would tell Mother and the rest of the family. Mother would be so proud...and Father would have been too! He would really be the man of the family now!

Roscoe glanced around to find his mother among the chattering crowd.

"There she is, talking to Mr. Possum," he said, starting to walk towards her, but halting as Mr. Beaver laid his hand on Roscoe's arm.

"Well, they seem to be having a little discussion, so why don't we wait a while. Meantime, we can go over some of the things you'd be doing."

Mrs. Mouse was indeed in deep conversation with Mr. Possum. Roscoe would have been surprised to know that he was a major subject of their talk.

"I'm not sure if you really understand the expenses of sending Roscoe to school in town," began Mr. Possum.

"Oh, I have a pretty good idea," said Mother Mouse, "Father went over all of that before he passed away." She smiled at Mr. Possum a bit sadly. "Father always intended for them to have a good education, and he always put something away. I have not touched that money -- it's still there for the children's educations. If only he could be here now," she sighed.

Mr. Possum responded very gently, for he knew that Mother Mouse still felt her loss keenly. "I'm sorry he's gone. He was a close friend of mine, you know. And I don't want to see his family suffering hardship because he's no longer here to take care of things himself. So I just want you to come to me if you need to." He waved aside Mrs. Mouse's protestations and expressions of gratitude.

"I can't begin to thank you. I've heard what you've done for the Moles, " she added confidentially, "and I think it's absolutely wonderful."

"Oh," scoffed Mr. Possum, embarrassed to have his good deeds known by all, "I did that for myself. I got tired of always having to set up Wally's tent for him on the camping trips -- that boy is all thumbs. Now old Mole will have to see to it himself." They both laughed.

"And speaking of helping your neighbor," continued Mr. Possum, "you've done both Muskrat and me a great favor. When you told me of his skills, I thought I was just doing a kindness by having him up to the house to redo some cabinets and furniture."

"Has it worked out well?"

"I'll say! After the work was completed I was so ashamed at how little I had offered for the job, that I increased the amount and embarrassed Muskrat no end!"

Mother laughed. "He is a very modest man, Mr. Possum, and very business-like. You probably upset his accounting!"

"Well, after seeing the project he was working on -- that is, some of his other work, I realized there was much more I wanted to have him do."

"What project is he working on?"

But Mr. Possum became suddenly reticent and looked around vaguely. He seemed relieved when he noticed Roscoe.

"I think your eldest boy wants to talk to you -- he's over there with Beaver, and it looks like he's wearing a hole in the ground the way he's shuffling around and looking over here."

With one more grateful smile, Mother Mouse wove her way through the knots of adults and children and soon was listening to Roscoe's explanation of Mr. Beaver's offer, the recounting of which was interspersed with excited exclamations and pleas for her permission.

Mother looked at Mr. Beaver over Roscoe's head and they exchanged nods. Roscoe glanced at each of them. "I can, then? Oh, thank you, Mother! Thanks, Mr. Beaver." In a flash he was gone to inform Sam of his good fortune, that he had a "real job", and to bask in the admiration of his friends.

What good friends we have! thought Mother Mouse. How would we have made it without them?

"Mother!" Roberta's voice interrupted her musings. "Didn't you hear me calling? The Muskrats are here now so we're going to give Skitch his presents. Hurry!"

Mother brought her thoughts back to the picnic and joined the group clustered around little Skitch.

"Here we go, Mrs. Mouse," said Father Mole, spreading a quilt over the old log. "You sit right down there and hold the baby, and then we can all see."

Mother took Skitch from Roberta's willing arms, then glanced at the gifts piled about her feet.

"Oh," said Annie, "I wish I was a baby and getting all those presents."

Little Skitch was dear to everyone and their relief at his survival was expressed in the gifts they had bestowed on him.

Mother looked up. Mrs. Beaver was talking in a low voice to Mrs. Rabbit.

"And then he said, 'It's not over yet, Mother," and my heart had just stopped, I know it. And off they rushed -"

"Hush, Mother," said Father Beaver. "Everyone knows what happened, we're all just glad he's safe and sound."

Mother Mouse smiled. "We can't hear it often enough. What would we have done if you hadn't been there?"

Father Beaver looked embarrassed, but pleased with Mrs. Mouse's comment.

"Okay, well," he mumbled, "let's get on with it.

"Ours first, please!" cried Franklin. "Mother wove it and Father finished it, but Molly and Thad and I collected all the reeds."

Mother looked again at the gifts, and singled out the reed basket. Holding it up, it became apparent there were two holes in the side of the tightly woven reeds, and handles had been attached at the top.

"It's a swing!" said Molly excitedly. "Mother wove them nice and tight and Skitch can sit in it and put his legs through the holes and Father is going to come and tie it up to the tree in your yard."

"Father said 'Maybe it will keep the young fellow out of mischief,'" offered Thaddeus.

Father Beaver blushed furiously and swore to himself to watch his conversation around the children in the future, but Mother Mouse only laughed.

"Let's hope so!" she gaily exclaimed.

There were quite a few chuckles when the Possums' gift was opened: a complete little sailor's outfit, including a jaunty cap. Mrs. Squirrel had baked nut fudge which Skitch immediately dove into. Mrs. Rabbit provided him with an array of stuffed toys which all the Rabbit daughters had helped to sew. The Hedgehog family presented Skitch with a brand new mattress stuffed with soft moss that they had collected in the woods.

Roberta had knitted Skitch a very long woolen scarf, causing a ripple of amusement in those gathered around.

"Well, I wasn't sure when I would get it finished, so I thought it better be something for winter just in case," she declared matter-of-factly.

Skitch wrapped it around his neck, with the balance hanging down back and front.

"It's sure long enough," frowned Megan Squirrel.

"All the better for him to grow into," hastily interjected her mother, with a stern look at her outspoken daughter. "And very practical," she added.

Roberta beamed.

When Sarah's pillow cover was revealed it elicited much admiration from the mothers, who crowded around to inspect her needlework and exclaim over the joyful explosion of birds and bees and butterflies that covered its surface.

"What beautiful work, Sarah!" said Mrs. Possum. "You must be very proud." Sarah smiled happily at the attention her work had drawn.

"You should enter your needlework in the fair, Sarah," said Mrs. Squirrel, then looked around in surprise at the amused groans around her.

Mrs. Mole cleared her throat and Mrs. Mouse gave her her full attention.

"Our gift is really more for you," she said softly, "rather than Skitch." And she presented Mother with a beautiful little figurine carved from the rock Mr. Mole had mined for so long.

"Oh!" breathed Mother, holding the beautiful object carefully in her hand so everyone could see.

"Why, it's Skitch, Mother!" cried Sarah excitedly. "It looks just like him!"

And so it did, catching him in a pose and with an expression so typical of him that there could be no doubt. Mother looked at Mr. Mole.

"How can I ever thank you for this?" she said.

Mr. Possum looked over at his newly hired manager with great respect in his eyes.

Everyone turned at the squeaking and rattling which came from the woods, as Roscoe and Sam emerged pulling the wagon they had made for Skitch.

"I told you we needed to oil the wheels," grumbled Sam, "and I know that back one has to be tightened. But, no, you were in such a rush -"

"Oh, hush, Sam," said Roscoe, smiling at the group of people awaiting their arrival. "We'll fix it later. Let's just give it to him, okay?"

Sam forgot his disgruntlement when he saw Skitch's response, for the baby slipped from his mother's lap and ran awkwardly towards his new toy.

"Voom! Voom!" he said.

"Yes, 'voom, voom'" laughed Roscoe, lifting him into the wagon and pulling him the rest of the way.

Taking advantage of the fact that everyone's attention was drawn to Skitch for the moment, Mr. Muskrat spoke quietly to Nick and Ned, who slipped off to their wagon. They returned, panting, carrying a large and obviously heavy wooden chest, which they placed with some relief at Mother's feet.

Mother Mouse looked up to see Mr. Muskrat's twinkling eyes.

"Just a little something from all of us," he nodded, "to say 'thank you.'"

Mother Mouse was speechless.

She ran her hand over the smooth sides of the chest and fingered the ornate clasp and lock. But her eyes were riveted, as were those of the others who had drifted back to see, on the elaborate carving on the lid.

A large oval wreath of roses, lilies, and daisies was intertwined with ivy, and enclosed raised letters carved in a handsome script.

"The Mouse Family," read Mother.

"For your keepsakes, ma'am," said Father Muskrat.

"I don't know how to thank you," stammered Mother, looking up, then down again at the beautiful chest. She could not keep her hands from tracing the flowing lines and exquisite woodwork.

The Mouse children were silenced by the gift and hovered around Mother and the chest, almost afraid to touch it.

Mother Mouse felt a deep joy inside. How connected everything was! She was in awe at the sudden awareness of the interrelationship of events that ran as a deep and mysterious undercurrent to their everyday lives.

Last Christmas her children had opened their hearts and home to the Muskrat family, which had led to Mr. Muskrat obtaining work in the village; even "Roberta's fire" (which was how the family would always remember it) had led indirectly to Mr. Muskrat making this chest for her. But the circle kept growing, and now, because of all the work Mr. Muskrat had, more orders than he could fill on his own, Joelle would be able to continue her education and go off to the town school with Roscoe.

Tears welled in her eyes, but she wiped them quickly away. Her thoughts were her own, and private, and she had no wish to share them now. She thought of how fortunate she was that her life was so full of everyday magic. Her mind fastened again on the events around her, but the joyful feeling remained.

And then the feast began, all partaking, with exclamations of pleasure and surprise, requests for recipes and promises for gifts of special dishes at Christmas. Even with all the food consumed, the talk continued to flow freely. The children dashed from one family's spread to another, stuffing themselves outrageously, with only half-hearted warnings from parents who resigned themselves to dealing with middle-of-the-night stomachaches.

By late afternoon, the dishes and quilts and tablecloths were being packed up in baskets and hampers. Some of the picnickers were beginning to talk of the following day's work, while others were looking tired and donning wraps as the air began to cool in the shadow of the large trees, and children were beginning to get sleepy and a little cranky.

"Time to load up," announced Father Beaver, and all followed suit willingly. The party had been splendid, but now they yearned for home and hearth.

"At least we can all fit in the cart, now," nodded

Father Beaver to Mrs. Mouse. "The Muskrats are bringing your hampers, and will drop them off at your gate."

"Where's Skitch?" inquired Mother, looking around her. There was always a moment of panic now when he was not directly in her sight.

"Over here," called Roscoe. "He won't move."

Seated in the wagon with his sailor's cap perched over one ear and Roberta's scarf ends trailing behind him, Skitch refused to budge. Facing forward, he pointed his finger straight ahead.

"Go!" he commanded.

"That's okay, Mother, I'll pull him home," said Roscoe, after Mother stood looking at the baby in exasperation, breathless with her struggles to lift Skitch out of the wagon while he held on tightly to each side and yelled at the top of his voice.

"Are you sure, Roscoe?" said Mother with a frown. "It's getting late and it's quite a distance."

"I'm sure, Mother," said Roscoe loftily. "You just take the little ones and go on in Mr. Beaver's cart."

Hiding a smile at the reference to Sarah, Roberta and Sam, Mother agreed, and soon they were trundling down the road and waving to Roscoe who had started out with Skitch.

The carts disappeared from sight and the laughter and happy calls faded in the distance. Roscoe plodded along, Skitch behind him in the wagon, now and then squeaking out instructions.

"Go, Woscoe, go!" "Voom! Voom!"

Roscoe smiled back at him. "You're lucky it's your birthday, fur ball!" he teased.

Roscoe ambled on, glad to be alone and have the woods to himself. School would be starting again in a while. He would be working for Mr. Beaver until then, helping him clear out the streambeds. Then school, and hard work, for it was his last session.

He was a little anxious about going away to school in town. He would really have to buckle down; he didn't want to seem like a dumb "country mouse" when he got there. At least he wouldn't be alone; Joelle and Homer would be going off to town as well. And he would still be helping Mr. Beaver and keeping up with his chores.

He sighed and looked around.

He certainly wouldn't have as much time to play in the woods. Mr. Hedgehog said they would be doing a lot more work in here now, fixing up the old overgrown pavilion, clearing more of the paths. Mrs. Hedgehog would have a cleared sunlit place to grow her herbs and medicinal plants to keep up with Dr. Raccoon's orders. A lot of the underbrush would be cut down and removed.

It would look nicer, thought Roscoe, but it wouldn't be quite as much fun.

Part of the attraction of the woods had been the hidden places that one stumbled upon, revealed only to a chosen few. Places where the shrubbery and vines had grown into almost impenetrable thickets, but, once you were through, opened onto little glades or ponds.

Probably the old tree would have to come down, thought Roscoe, gazing up through its leafy branches.

His favorite Robin Hood tree.

Many arrows had been shot from its branches, many daring deeds performed under its boughs. But it was dying, its branches dry and brittle, even refusing to leaf any longer.

Roscoe smiled as he followed the curve of the path.

Here was the spot he had come upon the Hallowe'en ghost, and ahead the tall iron fence. Robbie had watched him through the bars and had gone through a few moments of panic when he couldn't withdraw his head as easily as he had inserted it between the rungs. His cries had temporarily outstripped the 'ghost's' in spine-tingling terror.

They were out on the open road now. Roscoe glanced back at Skitch, who was still chattering quietly to himself and waving at birds and flowers. Roscoe was not sure his little brother made any distinction between the two. The sun was lower now, sending long, streaming rays across the meadow.

They passed the Hedgehogs' and Roscoe glanced up at the Possums' big house on the hill. Its many windows glowed with evening lamp light.

Trudging along, he realized that the wagon wheels were squeaking, as Sam had said, but it was only a slight sound and a sort of comforting accompaniment to their journey. He continued down the road that he had traversed many times before, but usually in a rush to get home on time.

I've seen the meadow so many times, thought Roscoe, but I didn't realize how pretty it was.

Although he knew his sisters and Sam played there, it was where Father had found him, and he had not been able to go there since.

*I've seen the meadow so many times, thought Roscoe, but I didn't realize how pretty it was.*

From here on, he thought, when I see this meadow I will choose to remember Father's happiness when he found me, and the love that sent him out in that storm to find me. He paused a moment to admire the golden grasses and wildflowers, brilliant in the late sunlight, then started up again.

Around another curve, and he could see a little cluster of houses, growing in size slowly as he walked on.

There, there was his house, lights on. Wisps of smoke rose from Wally's chimney. They must have started a fire already.

Mother would have cocoa for him when he got home, he thought with satisfaction.

By the time he was on the last leg of the trip home, the stars were already beginning to peek out of a sky still greenish-gold from the setting sun. He looked back again at Skitch. No wonder he hadn't heard anything from him -- Skitch was curled up in the wagon sound asleep, the long scarf bunched around him, and his sailor's cap in one little paw.

Now he was almost home.

There was his fence, and now the gate. Open the gate, pull Skitch through and latch it again.

The light was on in Sam's room -- he was probably reading. Sarah would be in the kitchen with mother, ready with cocoa and muffins and lots of butter and honey. From the upstairs window light, he could tell that Roberta was in her bedroom. Sarah had pestered her that afternoon with reminders that it was her turn to clean the room. Roberta had promised she would do it as soon as she got home.

At the sound of the little wagon on the paving stones, the front door opened and Mother appeared. Warm light glowed from inside the house and he could smell the muffins and cocoa. Mother was coming out to get little Skitch now.

He looked around him. The big tree which would soon hold Skitch's swing, the low wall between the Moles' house and theirs, the roses all in full bloom now on the fence, then Mother's welcoming face.

He smiled at her. It was good to be home.

# *ABOUT THE AUTHOR*

Dr. Karyl Hall retired to Carmel, California after thirty years as a research psychologist. She wrote grant applications and published research in the medical field, a world away from children's stories! Karyl grew up in the Carmel area, to which she credits her active fantasy life. Her other children's book (which is really for adults, too) is *Gnome Alone in Carmel,* based on a "true" story.

Karyl and her co-author Carolyn Graham, who also created the cover art, have been friends for eons.

And Natalie Bieser, the artist who created the wonderful inside illustrations, lives in Santa Fe, New Mexico.

You may email Karyl at Hallnelson@comcast.net or contact her via snailmail at PO Box 4582, Carmel, CA 93921.

SETON
PUBLISHING

www.ingramcontent.com/pod-product-compliance
Lightning Source LLC
Chambersburg PA
CBHW030338310726
48979CB00001B/91
*9781732545007*